S.G.POTTS

Abigail's Gift

S.G. POTTS

Abigail's Gift

EGMONT

EGMONT

We bring stories to life

First published 2006
by Egmont UK Limited
239 Kensington High Street
London W8 6SA

ISBN 978 1 4052 0762 1
ISBN 1 4052 0762 0

1 3 5 7 9 10 8 6 4 2

A CIP catalogue record for this title is available from the British Library

Typeset by Avon DataSet Ltd, Bidford on Avon, Warwickshire
Printed and bound in Great Britain by the CPI Group

For My Mother

Chapter 1

It is a velvet night – windless, warm and still – and we drift, Calum and I, in his father's old boat, on the waters of Bloody Bay. We sprawl, he in the bow, me in the stern. The lines between us are unattended, for the fishing is fruitless tonight.

I have never known such darkness. There is no moon, and behind us the low cliffs on the Mull shore shield the lights of Tobermory from view. The water is flat, utterly untroubled by breeze: there is magic in the air.

I feel the boat move as Calum stirs. I look over to the pale blur of his face and see him smile. 'Can you hear it?' he whispers, as if to speak out loud would break the spell.

I close my eyes. It makes no difference. 'Hear what?'

'This. Listen.'

I let a long moment pass. 'I hear nothing.'

'You have no soul,' he laughs. 'I hear a still and starless night. I hear peace, and uncaught fish laughing at us. I hear lobsters sing.'

And now *I* hear something. A breath in the darkness, out in the waters of the Sound, not far off. I look up past Calum, over the bows. And then I see it: a rocket, deep in the water, trailing brilliant yellow and glowing green stars as it hurtles towards the boat. I start and sit suddenly upright.

I grasp Calum's arm. I point and hiss, 'A water-horse!' Calum turns, lazily, slowly, as if he no longer believes in the mythical creature he has told me all about, a creature that rises out of the water to take the unwary.

The water-horse surges up from the depths, till it bursts from the surface right beside the boat in a shower of glowing spray. I stifle a scream. There is a gust of breath, and a boil of water when the creature dives again, as surprised by us as we were

– or I was – by it. I catch a glimpse of flipper, and the fishy waft left hanging in the air around us is unmistakable.

'Water-horse indeed!' laughs Calum. 'It's a seal, Morag. Nothing more. A selkie.' He runs his fingers through the water. The same yellow-green lights sparkle and twirl, and sparkle brighter the faster he moves his hands. 'A big grey seal, moving quickly to raise such phosphorescence. Chasing a fish, I'll swear. And by the smell of his breath he's caught more than we have tonight.'

He takes up the oars. 'Come,' he says. 'We've endured enough taunting by these fish for one night.' He turns the boat and we paddle gently towards the shore.

Abigail stood at the stern of the CalMac Ferry, watching the white wake stretch arrow-straight back up the Sound of Mull as the ship sped south-east to Oban and the start of the long drive home. The hills on either side hunkered close and dark right up to the water's edge, though their summits were again swathed in cloud. She couldn't see Ben Mor at all, set back as it was from the shore. She'd only seen it once in the entire two weeks, and that was from the ferry, before all the rain came.

Naomi looked from one side of the Sound to the other, and turned to Abigail. 'Dull *dull* DULL! There's only one word to rhyme with Mull. I promise you if you ever persuade them to take us to Scotland on holiday again I will kill you. Slowly and *very* horribly. Next year I want sunshine, and warm water to swim in, and hot sand to lie on and –'

'– Italian boys to gawp at,' Abigail broke in.

'Why not? Italian, or Spanish, or French.'

'Or German.'

Naomi shook her head. 'Not my type. Danish maybe. Or Dutch.'

'You don't speak Dutch.'

'We could communicate.'

4

Abigail stifled a laugh. Naomi whirled round. 'God knows how I didn't go out of my mind with boredom on that boggy island.'

'I wasn't bored.'

'But you're weird. Everyone knows that.'

Suppressed laughter died in Abigail's throat. 'I don't,' she said, dry-mouthed.

'But that's because you *are* weird. Tramping over empty beaches by a freezing cold sea . . . Squelching across muddy moors . . . Poring over museum junk . . . in the rain.'

'But I liked it. All of it. Even the rain.'

'And the midges?'

'OK. Maybe not them.'

Naomi waved at the misty hills. 'Look at it. Even now, when we're going home, it's dull. And it's *still* raining. I'm going inside.' And she stomped off to the cafeteria.

Abigail was glad to be left alone, alone with her sadness at leaving this place. From the moment of arrival she'd felt an affinity, a familiarity, a sense of *belonging* here that she could not explain to herself, never mind Naomi. If this was weirdness – or worse – then let them all sneer, her sister and the rest. She watched Duart Castle glide by on the starboard side and Lismore lighthouse to port, and then, as the ship entered Oban Bay and approached the harbour wharves, she moved forward to the bows.

❧

As the huge grey vessel inches forward into the windswept harbour, the arc lights on the quayside illuminate the driving rain then suddenly cut out, plunging the entire pier into impenetrable darkness. Captain Parker steps up to the radar screens.

'They're testing us, Number One.'

'Sir?'

'First they cancel the tugs, then they black out the wharf. They want to see us dock her blind.' He turns to other officers, standing quietly at their instruments. 'Both engines ahead, dead slow. Hold this course.'

'Aye aye, sir,' replies the helmsman, calmer than he

has any right to be, given that he's at the wheel of the Navy's newest ship. He can't see a thing, and there's a harbour wall somewhere dead ahead.

The captain turns back to me. 'Take her in, Number One.'

'Aye aye, sir.' I swallow hard and bend over the radar screen to hide my tumbling fears. If I prang this ship it'll be a court martial for sure, and I'll never make captain. I study the mess of blips on the screen, the anemometer readings of wind force and direction, the tiny numbers which tell where we are, how fast we're going, and how long till disaster. I look at the helmsman. 'Hold this course,' I tell him.

'Aye aye, ma'am.'

My eyes flit from screen to screen and dial to dial. There's no point looking outside. Unless . . .

'Mr Hardy?'

'Ma'am?'

'Night-sight goggles, if you please.' Behind me the captain smiles. He thinks I don't notice. I stride to the port end of the bridge and step outside. Rain hits me like a water cannon. It's hard to see where the water ends and the quay begins, but when I raise the goggles I can see the tiny figures pacing about atop the quay.

I step back inside. 'Starboard engine ahead dead slow. Stop port engine.' The helmsman looks at me. 'Let her come up into the wind, helmsman.'

'Aye aye, ma'am.' He sounds nervous too.

'Stop both engines.' There's an eerie silence on the bridge, made all the deeper by the shrieking of the wind and the drumming of the rain.

'Engines astern, ma'am?'

'If I want astern I shall ask for it, Mr Hardy. I'm letting the wind take her in.' And it does. Fifty thousand tons of warship is pushed sideways, inch by inch, foot by foot, towards the wharf, where she touches so gently the only way to tell we're alongside is to step outside and look down.

'Make fast bow and stern,' I order. The lights snap on and I slowly let out a long-held sigh of relief. All around I hear my fellow officers do the same.

There's a tap on my shoulder. 'Well done, Number One. Well done, indeed!'

Abigail's exasperated father tapped her shoulder. 'Found you, Miss Stowaway. Didn't you hear the announcements? We're supposed to be on the car deck.'

Abigail, who'd been bent over the ship's side rail, straining to watch the docking procedure, straightened up and stepped down. 'But this is the best part.' She looked around the deck, as if to say farewell to the ship. Moments ago it had been, however briefly, her first command; now it was just a car ferry again.

Her father took her arm and hustled her towards the nearest door, where the foot passengers stood around in clusters, blocking their way. 'Mum and Naomi are already down there,' he said. She could tell he was working to suppress his irritation. 'I had to fight my way up against the crowds to find you.'

She followed him down the crowded staircase.

Eventually they reached the car deck, packed with cars and lorries and smelling of diesel, salt water and fish. Far ahead the bow doors opened, letting in a flood of grey daylight. She got into the car.

'Where were you this time?' her mother asked at last. She didn't turn round.

Abigail's father spoke before she could reply. 'I found her on the side deck, hanging off the railing like a monkey.'

Her mother turned round. 'In your head, I meant, Abby. Where did you go in your head?'

Abigail knew from experience it was better not to answer directly. 'I just wanted to see the ship dock, Mum. That's all, honest.'

Her mother turned round to face ahead again. 'The holiday's over, Abby. There'll be no room for daydreams at your new school. Ask Naomi.'

Naomi grunted. 'There's weirdo kids in every class. Don't be the weirdo in yours. It'll be *soooo* embarrassing.'

Abigail looked at her. 'Embarrassing for me or for you?'

'Don't you two start,' said Dad. 'We've a long drive ahead.' There was a rustling in the front seat, and

Abigail's mother's hand stretched back, beside the head rest. The fingers opened to reveal a clump of peanuts. 'Monkey nuts,' she said, her voice lighter now. 'Salted, for sea-monkeys.'

Abigail reached forward and picked up a nut between her thumb and first finger. She puckered her lips and took the nut between them, running it around her gums with increasingly loud monkey noises.

'For God's sake!' hissed Naomi. She snapped on her Walkman. 'Will you *ever* grow up?'

Abigail's monkey noises grew louder and shriller. She bounced up and down in her seat and curled back her monkey lips to show her monkey teeth, then pushed her monkey arms across to pat Naomi's shoulder with the back of her hand.

'Ahem!' coughed her father. Abby looked up. A family in the next car were pointing at Abigail and laughing. She abruptly gave up her monkey impression and sank down in her seat until their car had moved ahead. *It only takes a moment*, she thought. *Do anything different and you're branded a weirdo. Branded for life.*

The morning sun rises through a cloudless sky and a fresh breeze tugs at my hair and my long heavy skirt as I step over the bouldered shore, following Calum. We each carry a heavy basket half-full of kelp. Behind us, up on the pier, the women of Croig boil up a big vat of porridge on an open fire.

Calum pauses to point at the water's edge where the kelp clumps thickly at a small headland. 'There,' he says. 'Let's try there.' He hitches his basket higher on his shoulders and sets off. I follow his wet boot prints on the stones.

When Calum stops again I see a red-brown shape emerge from the water and move on to the drying kelp. 'Water-dog!' I whisper. A little flock of oystercatchers takes flight at the otter's approach. Their long thin bills and slender feet flash scarlet amid the black and white beating of their wings. '*Bi glic!*' they call in a burbling cadence, as of a brook. '*Bi glic!*'

The otter ignores them, for it has a fish in its mouth, still flapping feebly. It drops the fish on the kelp to stare at us, and when Calum steps forward it huffs in irritation, takes up its prey, and slips back into the water, to swim past the point and out of our sight.

We approach the piles of kelp. Fish scales glisten silver where the otter had stopped. I put down my basket and begin to fill it with all the weeds of the sea: dulse and tangle, sea-lettuce, coral weed, and every kind of wrack – channelled wrack, knotted wrack, toothed wrack and my favourite, bladderwrack, with air bubbles to pop when it dries out. I load heavy clumps into the basket.

'What do they do with it?' I ask.

'They dry it in the sun, then burn it. They spread the ash on their fields as fertiliser.'

'So we're taking from the sea to give to the land,' I say, pleased with myself.

'No. We take what the sea gives free, to put

on someone *else's* land. The most valuable part of it never sees the land at all. It is used to make soap or glass. *Barr oir a' cuartachadh Eilean Muile.* And that is why we have less of it to spread on our own land.'

'Is there less seaweed this year?'

'That's what the old ones say.' He lifts another clump and, seeing his own basket is full, he tosses it into mine. 'But they say so every year at this time. That is why they make the porridge.'

It is then I smell the cow boat. I stand and look across the water to Coll and Tiree. The breeze has whipped mare's tails off the tops of the deep-blue waves. A lumbering boat wallows in the swell, its stumpy mast tracing an arc as it runs before the wind towards us and the tiny harbour at Croig. A patched tan sail bellies out ahead, drawing the boat on.

Calum holds his nose and grimaces. 'Here come the cattle,' he says. And now the wind brings, as well as the smell, the terrified lowing of

14

the animals packed on the pitching deck.

As we lug our laden baskets back towards the pier, the boat draws close to shore and takes in sail. We watch as it rounds up into the wind and lets go its anchor in the shelter of the harbour's mouth. The smell and sound and sight of the packed black cattle is powerful, but we must turn away as we totter over wobbling boulders with our loads.

We're past the tide line when we hear behind us, above the general lowing of the herd and the gruff shouts of the crew, a single, higher, frightened cow-call, and then a huge splash as the first beast is thrown overboard. The startled animal surfaces, turns a full circle, and then, when it finds it can swim, strikes out for the shelving sandy beach inside the pier. It is soon followed by another and another as the herd is tossed, cow by cow, into the sea to swim ashore, the salt water cleaning the matted muck from their thick black coats.

I lower my basket beside the others on the pier.

A heavyset man with something of Calum in the line of his jaw counts up the total. 'Is that all?' he asks brusquely.

Calum nods. 'We can scrape together another basket, perhaps two, Uncle Murdo, but –'

'No matter. We take what we can get.' He turns, as if seeing me for the first time. 'And how is Morag?'

'I'm well, Mr Munro.'

'And your mother? We see her so little.'

'She is well too, sir.'

'Tell her I was asking after her.'

'I will,' I tell him. *I won't*, I tell myself. *It'll only make her angry*. It always makes her angry to hear of Murdo's interest in her.

One of the women on the pier tastes the porridge, then hands her ladle to those nearby. They nod at each other, then call across to their menfolk, busy mending nets and creels at the water's edge.

Two men lift the heavy vat and lead the way

along the path towards a small cliff near the entrance to the bay. The rest follow. Calum looks to his uncle. 'May we go?'

'Aye. Go if you must, superstitious nonsense that it is. What a waste of good oats! And when you return you will load these baskets on to the cart,' he calls after us.

We track the porridge people at a respectful distance. They stop where the path approaches most closely the top of the cliff, where they set down the vat. One of the women starts singing in Gaelic. I cannot make out the words, though I know the tune. The other women join in the chorus while the men lift and upturn the vat, sending a great gloopy mass of porridge down the cliff, to spatter the kelpy rocks and splash into the sea. Startled gulls rise up then plummet down to feast on the sticky mess.

Calum turns to me with a grin. 'You're an otter, a water-dog, minding your own business, tucking into a herring, when a ton of hot porridge falls from the sky and hammers you on to the rocks. What do you say?'

'That people are strange creatures and I will never understand them. Why do they do it?'

'They're making the sea an offering. We grow oats to make porridge, to make a gift from the land to the sea, in the hope that she will return it to us in a harvest of kelp —'

'Which we take for fertiliser, to raise our crops of corn and wheat . . . and oats —'

'So completing another turn in the circle of life.'

'Except now we break the circle by selling the kelp.' There is a rare flash of anger in his eyes and an unfamiliar hardness in his voice. 'So our land, which was never rich, grows a little poorer year by year, and we can raise less food, so we must instead raise money by selling the kelp. By the time I come of age my land will be nothing but dust, and fit to grow nothing but turnips.'

Calum turns away to look back to the pier.

'We must return to load the cart. Uncle Murdo's not a patient man.'

I turn too, and together we retrace our steps. Behind us the old people of Croig linger on the clifftop, laughing and chatting in both English and Gaelic.

In the bay the last cow has swam ashore, and the crew of the cow boat smoke pipes on deck. The animals huddle above the tide line, dripping water, steaming in the sunlight, and nosing among the rocks for any edible grass. A man and boy tend them, herding them with sticks and examining their flanks for wounds. Two eager black and white dogs look on.

I catch Calum watching them. 'Would you be a drover?' I ask him.

He beams. 'I would. Think of it: a different campsite every night, a different landscape every day. Watching for reivers and thieves. Living by your wits. And at the end of it all, a big purse of money to bring safely home.' We've reached the cart, and together we bend to lift the first basket. Calum's uncle takes it from us.

'But it's such a distance,' I say, as we reach for the next basket.

It's not Calum but his uncle who replies. 'To Falkirk? Aye, but most don't go that far. They sell the beasts at Crieff or hand them over at Oban. It's still a hard life.'

Calum looks up brightly. 'Yes, Uncle Murdo.' There's a question in his face.

Murdo studies him. 'Are you man enough yet?'

Calum nods vigorously. 'I am sure of it.'

Murdo pauses. 'Not this time.'

Calum reaches for the next basket. 'But soon?'

'Perhaps.'

I grasp the basket handle and meet his eye. 'Can Morag come?' Calum asks.

Murdo splutters out a cruel laugh and turns away. 'Is *she* man enough?'

I look again at Calum. He lets go of his handle, allowing me to take them both. I plant my feet. When Murdo has turned back to face me I lift the basket, trying not to let the strain show. My legs quiver and something hurts behind one knee, but the basket begins to rise. I push harder, and grip tighter, till the basket passes my hips and is now at my waist. I strain again, and feel my face going red. Murdo stands above me, looking down. He does not help. He does not speak. But he is no longer laughing. I drop the basket on the cart with a grunt. 'I wouldn't stop at Crieff or even Falkirk,' I tell them both. 'I'll go all the way. All the way to London.'

I stare at the pock-marked neck of the driver in the seat in front of me. Beside him the officer reaches inside his overcoat. On either side of me the Gestapo men sit totally still and utterly silent.

How did they know? I ask myself. Who else have

they caught? Were we betrayed?

The officer turns to me and opens a silver cigarette case. I study his face. Is he a torturer? How far will he go? 'Zigaretten, Fraulein?' he asks with a cold, hard smile, and I know. He'll go as far he has to.

I shake my head, remembering my SOE training at Arisaig. They'll offer you things, Maxwell had said. Chocolate, cigarettes, a shower. Never accept. However subtly, it makes you grateful. It makes you want to offer something in return. A name perhaps. A grid reference. A map. Give them nothing, however badly you might want it. Give them nothing at all.

'Nein, danke.' I say in my best German. 'Nicht rauchen.'

The cigarette case snaps shut and the officer's smile flashes off. He turns to face ahead . . .

Naomi dug her sister in the ribs and took one of the liquorice sticks her mother offered from the seat in front.

'*Nein, danke. Nicht rauchen,*' said Abigail.

Naomi shook her head. 'She's talking nonsense again, Mum.'

'That was German,' said her father. 'It means "I don't smoke". Where have you met German people offering you cigarettes, Abby?'

Naomi sniggered. 'In her dreams, Dad.' She turned to Abigail with a liquorice stick gripped between her teeth, and mimed the flicking of a lighter. 'Got a light, mate?

We finally halt just after dawn, and pull off the road into a compound of wire and fences, and searchlight towers standing high over miserable wooden huts. A prison camp. The still-silent Gestapo men lead me from the car and into the biggest building. The driver stays behind. Once inside there are curt exchanges in brisk, official German: names, dates, places. A back door is opened and another prisoner is half-led, half-carried

through. We recognise each other, though we pretend not to. Peter. His dull eyes and blood-matted hair, and the way he cannot walk, tell of the torture he's taken, and now I know how they found us. The Gestapo officer has heard my sharp intake of breath. It's all he needs. It's what he brought me here for.

A hundred miles on the car finally stopped at the kennels outside town. Barks and yapping filled the air. Mum strode up to the office building, chequebook in hand, while Dad stayed behind to arrange a space among the luggage in the back of the car. Within moments a familiar barking announced the arrival of a brindled dog, led by a handler.

'Muppet!' cried Abigail, as she spread her arms wide. The dog hesitated, looked to his handler as if to ask who these strangers were, then hurled himself forward in a tumult of barking and leaping and licking at faces. Dad took the tangled lead from the handler and reined in the whirlwind as best he could. 'Still nuts, I see,' he said.

The handler shrugged and smiled. 'You should see some of the others,' she said. She patted Muppet's head, then left. The dog stared after her longingly. 'I think he wants to stay here,' said Naomi.

'It's called Stockholm syndrome,' said Abigail. 'The attachment of a hostage to his captors.'

'I don't care what it's called,' said Dad. 'He's not staying here any longer. Not at ten pounds a day.'

I pick my way along the path on the hillside above Dervaig, towards the forest fence. There is a rickety gate, beyond which the path continues – but less well-trodden – between the trees, the last remnants of the ancient forest that once covered the island. The bright day dims greenly above me, and the windrush and bird song hush as I enter the cathedral of trees. Ahead of me is a clearing.

Two huge stones stand upright, taller than any man on Mull. Between them a third lies toppled, half-embedded in grass and pine needles. And on it, lost in thought, sits my mother.

I snap a twig underfoot to announce myself. She looks round, startled, and after an instant's hesitation she gives me a big wide smile.

'Morag!'

'I thought I would find you here.'

'It is the right kind of day to come.' She pats the lichen-coated stone beside her and I sit. I notice she's been making daisy chains. The white of the little flowers shows sharply against her smooth olive skin. She lays the flowers down and strokes the mossy surface between us.

'Who put the stones here?' I ask her. I've never thought to ask before.

'The ancient people. Many years ago.'

'Why?'

'It is not known, and perhaps never will be.'

I look up at the pillars towering either side

of me. 'It must have been something important to them.'

'Yes. You can feel that, even now.' She looks away into the distant green dimness. 'And for some of us there is still meaning here. Especially today.'

She suddenly turns to look at me again, and I think I see a glitter in her eyes before she blinks it away. 'Calum. Is he well?'

'He is. He grows stronger.' I blush, and now it is my turn to look away.

There's a silence. Her dark hair falls thickly forward, shielding her eyes. There is bitterness in her voice when she speaks. 'And Calum's uncle. Was *he* there?'

'He was.' I have never understood why she detests him so violently, but I cannot lie to her. 'He asked after you.'

She stands up sharply, crumpling the daisy chain and dropping it to the ground. 'Did he indeed?'

'I wasn't going to tell you.' I stoop to rescue the

crumpled flowers. 'But you asked.'

She circles the fallen stone in silence, and I watch her a while. When she passes before me again, I hold out a bundle. 'I have supper, Mother,' I tell her. She takes it, and unwraps the coarse cloth to uncover the lobster. It is not large but it will feed us tonight, together with the last of the winter potatoes. Neither of us knows what will feed us tomorrow.

She smiles at me, but from within her hidden place. I have to bring her out.

'I want to go droving,' I tell her.

It works. She whirls round, her eyes wide. 'What?' she demands.

'Mr Munro said Calum could go. So I asked if I might.'

'And?'

'He laughed at me. But I showed him I can do anything Calum can. I can herd cattle, and walk all day, and build a fire, and make a camp.' My mother stares at me. 'I can fight if I have to.'

'*No!* No, you may *not* go droving, however many lobsters you bring me.' And she turns and strides off, out of the clearing and into the wood.

❧

'Well?' Abigail's father drummed his fingers on the steering wheel. 'We can park and sit down in Burger King or KFC, or we can grab and go at the McDonald's drive-through.'

'The one thing I'm *not* doing after such a long drive is any cooking.' Mum was emphatic.

'Quite right. So come on, girls.'

Naomi and Abigail waited because neither wanted to go first, knowing the other would immediately contradict her. Abigail guessed what Naomi's choice would be. 'KFC,' she said innocently.

The momentary flash in Naomi's eyes told Abigail she'd guessed right. There was a pause before Naomi responded. 'Let's not sit down. We can't rescue Muppet after two weeks then lock him up in the car straight away.'

Dad flicked the indicator on and pulled off the road. 'OK then. McDonald's it is.' He drove up to the gaudy red and yellow cabin standing like an island in a black tarmac sea.

'A drove-through,' said Abigail to herself.

'What?' asked her sister.

'Nothing. I'm just not sure a poor cow that's been herded across the Highlands and Islands should end up in a bun in a bag for my tea.'

'Eh?'

'This is McDonald's, isn't it? Scottish meat. Scottish cows.'

'You really *are* nuts.'

'Decision time again,' said Dad as he wound down his window opposite the teenager in the kiosk.

Abigail leant forward and grinned at the gormless youth. 'I'll have the lobster, please.'

∽

I lay my sheepskin on the floor, between Fingal

and the fire. It's hard to find a place: too close to the fire and the sparks will strike to wake me with the smell of smouldering wool; too far away and I'll be shivering by dawn. Wherever I sleep there'll be Fingal, stretching in his dog dreams to scratch me with the rough skin of his pads.

Behind the screen Mother's already in bed, reading by a candle. I lie down and pull the other sheepskin over me. These skins are old and worn and smell too much of sheep, but they are warm, and tonight, with a good meal inside me, they will soon bring sleep.

The sackcloth curtain has fallen from the window, and through it I see the stars. Mother snuffs out her candle and now, in the deeper darkness, I study the constellations. I look for the hunter and his dog and wonder what tomorrow will bring. I look for the Bull and think of the drovers camping at Salen tonight. The last thing I hear, as sleep steals upon me, is the distant hoot of an owl.

Muppet weighed heavy on her legs as Abigail curled up in her bed, staring through the window opposite. She'd not drawn the curtains tonight.

A satellite tracked across the sky and aeroplane lights winked red and white in the flight lanes to the west. Abby ignored them as she rummaged in her memory for the names of stars and the shapes of constellations. 'There's Orion. The hunter,' she whispered to herself. 'And that's Sirius.' She stroked Muppet's ears. 'The Dog Star. One of those is Betelgeuse and one is Rigel, but I can never remember which one's which.' She sighed. 'Do they teach astronomy in school? Will I get a chance to learn about the stars?'

Abigail turned to the wardrobe where her new school uniform hung freshly pressed, and then to the desk where her bag bulged with books. 'Will I get a chance at all?'

Chapter 2

Naomi walked beside Abigail until they were out of sight of the house. Once they caught up with the first of Naomi's friends a subtle distance developed between the two sisters – a distance which widened as more friends joined, till Abby was walking alone.

The pavements were filling with kids, whose identical uniforms belied the huge differences between them. They approached the school gates from all directions, singly, in twos and threes, or in large turbulent groups, like minor streams and mighty rivers entering the great salt lake of the playground. *I'm a brook*, mused Abigail, *a babbling freshwater brook. And when I pass that gate I won't be a brook any more, just a bit more water running into the sea.* She stopped at the entrance, as other children flowed past her to join the hundreds already swirling round the yard. She took a deep breath and stepped forward.

⁊

Outside our croft I turn to plead with my mother, but she is unmovable. 'You must go,' she insists, and she indicates our tiny home on its hard-scratch land. 'If you are to escape this meagre life, you must learn. I teach you what and when I can but it is not enough, for I had too little teaching of my own.'

'But they ignore me,' I plead, though I know it is futile. 'And when they don't it is to call me names.'

'Who does?'

'All of them.' It is not true, and she knows it. I relent. 'All except Calum.'

'What names?'

'Spanish Morag. English Morag.'

'There are worse names. And there is some truth in each of these. Your Spanish blood is centuries old and now much diluted, but your English blood is more recent . . .' Her voice trails away and she reaches out for my red–brown hair.

All I know of my father is that he was once a soldier in an English regiment, stationed here on Mull to keep the fires of rebellion from sparking back into life. Silence clamps my mother's mouth if ever he is mentioned, silence I must break.

'*Witchy* Morag.' I know this will rouse her, though I will hear no more of my English blood.

'They call you that?'

'Yes.'

'Because of me?'

'Yes.'

There is a long silence, broken at last when she bids me sit on a bench beside the cottage door. She holds her arm against mine. Where I am pale and freckled she is a smooth hazelnut tan, and not from the sun, for she scarcely ventures out now.

'Look at you: you are as Celtic as any of those who taunt you, or these hills about us. I look different,' she says, as if it were not obvious. 'Whether, as some say, it is from the sailors of the Spanish Armada who were wrecked here centuries ago, I do not know. But the difference is enough.'

I stare at her. She's never spoken like this before. 'People want someone to blame when things go wrong. They cannot blame the powerful or the wealthy or the strong, because all they are left with is anger they cannot act on.'

She looks up, over the village of Dervaig, to the shore. Beyond it lie Coll and Tiree and beyond them the open Atlantic and the New World. She sighs. 'So they choose the weak. Usually old, always women, always alone. And to take a cat for company is enough to be damned.' She kicks at the loose earth under the bench. 'If the fish don't rise, it is the witch's curse. If the crops are blighted, 'tis the witch's doing. If the cow falls sick, or a boat goes down, it is the witch. Always the witch.

'And when they are sure enough, or angry enough, they will act. They will drag their victim before what they call a court – which never finds them innocent – and they will hang her, or burn her, or stone her till she is dead.

'They will feel better for a while, telling themselves they have lifted the curse. Until misfortune returns, as it always does, and they must look around for another victim.' She turns to me, takes my hands in her smooth brown grip, and holds me in her dark sad eyes. 'And not so long ago that victim would have been me.'

She releases me and abruptly stands up, determination written on her face. 'So you must study, and, you must learn, that you may find a different life where such deadly superstitions are but a distant memory.'

She turns to the cottage door, looking back only once, at the threshold, to make sure I am walking, as she now knows I will, towards school.

The teacher, Mrs Crawford, patrolled the rows of desks, pursued by thirty pairs of anxious eyes. But not by Abby's. Whatever she was watching, it wasn't in the room.

Mrs Crawford reached Abby's row and moved forward from the back wall, with smiles of encouragement for the nervous new pupils and the first words of warning for the boisterous ones. Eventually she stood at Abby's shoulder, awaiting a response.

Abigail didn't move. She didn't turn to see the teacher. She didn't speak to give her name. Mrs Crawford reached out towards her heedless shoulder.

Abby turned at the touch. The teacher smiled. 'We're taking names,' she said. 'What's yours?'

'M-M-M-Morag. Morag McGregor,' Abby stammered.

Mrs Crawford walked on to the next desk, studying her list. She stopped and turned, with a frown on her face. 'Are you sure? We don't have a Morag in this class. Perhaps you should be next door.'

Abby's attention was now fully in the room, and as she realised what she had done she blushed blood red. 'I'm – I'm sorry, Miss.' The heat rose in her face. 'I'm Abigail. Abigail Jones.'

A girl nearby – Elaine, Abby was soon to learn – nudged her desk-mate. 'What a weirdo!' she whispered.

Mrs Crawford tried to be kind. 'You're *quite* sure?'

Abby nodded, then lowered her head in case any tears came. It was the worst possible start, and she'd only herself to blame.

Dervaig's church bell sounds the hour, releasing us at last from the purgatory of a Latin class, made so much worse by its uselessness. I see no value in learning a language spoken by long-dead foreign conquerors – who *never* conquered Scotland – while our own living Gaelic tongue is suppressed in favour of English. So I block the words – *amo amas amat* – from my mind, and I wait until the schoolmaster dismisses us. And then I wait for the other pupils to leave before me. It gives them fewer opportunities to taunt me.

When it is quiet, and I judge it safe to leave, I collect my books and make for the door. No sooner am I through than I am grasped by my arm and pulled roughly aside. I raise my other arm, ready to strike, using my books as weapons and suddenly thankful for their weight. But then I see it is Calum who has gripped me and he holds a finger to his lips.

I follow him out of the building, into the lane beyond. We are almost running. When we are out of sight of prying eyes we halt, and he speaks at last.

'There's a bear!' he tells me excitedly. 'A bear, I tell you!'

'What?'

He grips my arm again. 'Come. I'll show you.' And we move on down the lane.

A little outside the village, on a rise

overlooking the deep inlet of the sea that is Loch a' Chumhainn, stand two horse-drawn caravans, brightly painted in unfamiliar designs. Between them is a wheeled cage, now empty.

Five hobbled horses wander the green, nibbling at the grass. Smoke rises behind one of the caravans, and from behind the other there emerges a troop of children, oddly garbed and talking a language I do not know.

To one side, away from the caravans and horses and tethered by a long chain, sits the biggest, fiercest beast I have ever seen. It moves its enormous head from side to side, sniffing the air and peering about through tiny eyes deeply embedded above a massive snout. When it stops moving its head and sniffs again, more loudly now, I am sure it is staring at me. I stiffen and halt, though Calum urges me on. 'They don't see well,' he reassures me. 'And this one's tame,' he says. 'It dances.'

The monster opens its jaws wide, exposing

huge fearsome teeth and a purple lolling tongue the size of a man's arm. 'It doesn't look tame to me,' I counter. 'And 'tis not I who'll be its dancing partner.' The jaws open wider yet, but in place of the roar I expect comes a long loud yawn, and the beast slumps forward, lays its head on its monstrous forepaws, and falls instantly asleep.

Calum smiles. 'Not even the last waltz?'

I smile back. 'Not even that.'

'Abby?' The television – a wildlife programme – drowned out her mother's voice. 'Abigail?'

Abby let the TV images slide past her unseeing eyes as she replayed the torments of the day on the screen in her head, again and again.

'*Abby!*'

'Yes, Mum?'

A scoosh of tyres on the tarmac outside became a scrunch as a car turned off the road and into the drive.

42

'So you're *not* a hologram after all! Lay the table would you? That's Dad back. And then, when you've found your tongue, you can tell us all about your first day at school.'

Abby turned the TV off, and as she placed the cutlery she listened to the familiar sequence of sounds: handbrake on, music – Tammy Wynette – off, engine off, car door clunks shut, scrunch of footsteps, house door swings open. Warm embrace, smothered kiss. 'Hello, love. Nice to be home.'

The table was set, the food ready, the moment not far off. Abby still didn't know what she was going to say or, worse, what Naomi would tell them.

Calum leads me across the machair grass at the head of Calgary Bay. Behind us stands the big house, all dark stone and white window frames. Fingal canters along ahead of us, drawn on to the dunes by the scent of rabbit. Beyond him spreads the wide sweep of white sand, half-freed of water as the tide ebbs towards the setting sun, whose low red rays flicker between the shadows of his loping legs. The surf is distant and gentle, there being little wind. It is a beautiful evening.

'Why is she so set against it?' asks Calum.

I shake my head, and step down from the last of the grass to the low dunes. 'I do not know. She used to go droving herself once.'

Calum jumps down behind me. 'Perhaps if my uncle –'

'No. I fear that if he asks she will never relent.'

Calum doesn't reply but stoops abruptly, then drops to his knees and scoops something out of the sand. I bend beside him. 'Give me your hand,' he urges, with a smile. I hold out my palm and he passes me an object which has the size and the roundness, though not the weight, of a pebble. Its leathered brown skin is puckered and salt-stained and scratched, but it sits snugly in the hollow of my hand, and something makes me curl my fingers around it.

'A molucca bean,' says Calum. 'They wash up here sometimes.'

'Wash up from where?'

He stands and points towards the sun, now setting amid a nest of purple clouds. 'From far over that horizon. The Caribbean Sea. It is a seed from a shore-side vine. They drop into those warm waters and drift across the ocean in the currents, to fetch up on beaches like this years later.'

I open my hand and stare at this modest but well-travelled nut as Calum continues. 'Their journey pickles them in brine, and cooks them in the sun, and even if it didn't they could never sprout on shores as cold as ours. But any bean lucky enough to strike land after so long a voyage must bear its share of good fortune. So it is a thing to be treasured. A charm.'

I hand it back to him. 'Then let the fortune be yours, since it was you that found it.'

He smiles, and slips the prodigal bean into my

pocket. 'If we are together, it does not matter which of us is bean-bearer: the good fortune will extend to us both.'

'And will we always be together?'

He stares at me and makes as if to reply, but no words come. And then he straightens, stands, and stares out to sea. 'Look!' he says as he points again.

Fingal pads across the still-wet strand, which is now painted over by the sunset's rainbow glow and reflecting the metallic colours of the sky. At each of his footfalls a disc of sand changes colour under his weight. Where it was light it darkens, and where dark it flares brighter. With every step circles of sand are transmuted into gold and silver, copper and pewter, but only for a moment, till Fingal lifts his leg and moves on. He strides on a stepping-stone trail, an alchemist hound whose enchanted feet turn Calgary sand into precious metal; but he has forgotten half the spell, so the transformation only endures in his presence.

Calum takes my hand. 'It is a powerful charm indeed if it also works on dogs,' he says.

ᕲ

'And then there was astronomy,' said Abigail brightly. She was talking so much her chips were going cold.

'Really?' her father asked. 'On your first day?'

'I learnt all about the stars. Well, I learnt a bit about a few of them, like Orion and Aldebaran and the Pleiades. And what a supernova is.'

Her father turned to Naomi. 'Things have changed, eh? Your first day was just maths tables and an old poem, wasn't it, Near-Miss?' Naomi frowned. She didn't know what to make of her sister's prattle.

Abigail's mother leaned forward and spoke with a cooler tone. 'But what did they learn about you?'

Abigail's barrage of chatter came to a sudden halt. She bent to her plate and cast a sidelong glance at her sister. Naomi opened her mouth to speak and Abby feared the worst, but all Naomi did was to silently mouth a single word: '*Weirdo.*'

Abby raised her head. 'I don't know what they learnt about me. They didn't say.'

༄

It is half-dark by the time the bear is put to dance. The inhabitants of Dervaig and Aros and Calgary are gathered round the green in little groups, all keeping a wary separation from the creature we have come to watch, which now slouches by its cage, grumpily aloof. I sit with my mother, who maintains as much distance from everyone else as they do from the bear.

A fiddler's note sounds over the crackling of the fire. The bear's keeper steps forward, dressed in a costume we have never seen, all covered with little bells. He holds his note, low and long, till the buzz of conversation stops. He stamps his foot. His shoe makes a hollow clacking sound and the bells tied round his knee jingle. He stamps again, and then again, establishing a rhythm, and the bear stirs, raising its heavy head to gaze around.

He continues stamping. The travelling children clap along, and slap the leather of their costumes. The keeper sounds the same low note again, but louder now, and the bear lets out a bellow, as if in answer, before shuffling awkwardly to its feet. It is moving faster now than at any time today, as if eager for what it knows will soon follow.

So I am alarmed to see the keeper stride his jingling way over to the bear to unclip his chain. A murmur goes round the crowd, and anxious mothers call their children closer.

The keeper sounds his fiddle note a third time. When it ends, he breaks into a jaunty reel and begins to dance around his creature, whose head and shoulders have begun to roll from side to side in time with the music.

The keeper calls, his fiddling faster, and the bear rises up on its hind legs to stand twice as tall as its whirling master. It raises its forepaws and bellows again, louder than before. Its teeth glint fiercely white in the firelight.

And then it begins to dance, stepping from leg to leg and turning a circle in the opposite way to its master. The children stop clapping to join hands and make a line, which the eldest leads off in a circling dance, enclosing their father the keeper as he whirls and spins. And at the centre of the circle, turning on the spot, orbited by his moon-keeper and his planet children, is the bellowing, stomping, dancing sun bear.

I look at my mother, and for the first time in many weeks I see her smile. Firelight gilds her cheeks and her eyes shine bright as she turns to me, reflecting my delight. She claps her hands together, high beside her face in what she calls the Spanish way. She laughs and I laugh back.

The music swells to a climax, then suddenly dies as the keeper flourishes his fiddle bow above his head. The bear drops to all fours and lowers his head, as if in a bow to his audience. The keeper and the children line up on either side of him and they all bow too. The keeper sweeps off his hat and steps forward. '*Danke, danke, meinen Herren und Damen*,' he entreats. '*Danke.*'

He extends his hat to a little group of Dervaigers on my right. No one offers him anything. He wipes the sweat from his brow and passes to the next group, trying to hide his disappointment.

'He little knows our poverty.' The voice beside me is Murdo. Neither of us had heard or seen his approach, so involved were we in the bear dance. My mother's smile has gone when she turns to him. She doesn't speak.

The keeper moves through the crowd towards us, repeating his futile '*Danke*', though the villagers have given him nothing to thank them for. My mother rummages deep in the pocket of her dress and beckons him over. She drops a coin I did not know she had into his hat. There is no clink because there are no other coins there. He bows his head. '*Danke, Fraulein*,' he says, as his face softens. '*Danke schön.*' And now, with an obvious effort, he continues in English. 'Many bears in Dervaig?' he asks, in a bid to understand the poor return on his efforts.

My mother's smile returns. 'Aye,' she says. 'Bears dance here all the time. People here are bored with them.'

He offers her a sad, defeated smile of his own and pockets the coin, then replaces his hat and returns to his unrewarded bear and disappointed children.

'Wait!' calls Murdo, as he steps out after him and dips his hand into a well-guarded pocket of his own. The keeper turns, and Murdo positions himself so that my mother can see as he drops a shiny silver shilling and two darker crowns on to the grateful man's hand.

My mother still doesn't say anything, but I see the feelings flit across her face. I know the coin she gave up must have been her last, and I know she wanted to shame the villagers into offering their own; but for Murdo to turn it round, and show her that though he spoke of poverty it did not apply to him, only upset her.

There is a tug on my skirt and I look down to see a small boy, one of the keeper's children. He looks from me to my mother, then points towards their horse-drawn wagon where a woman stands in front of a cooking fire, beckoning us forward.

❧

The low autumnal sun brought a brightness to the late afternoon sky when the grey tumbled clouds parted at last. The slanting rays were too weak to brighten the gloomy classroom, but they brought a little warmth to Abigail's heart. At the front of the classroom the teacher droned on, her drift long lost amid the maze of squiggles on the distant blackboard. Physics, or perhaps chemistry. It didn't matter: Abigail couldn't tell the difference.

She turned her face towards the window and, through it, the setting sun. Furtively she held her hands up, one behind the other, and moved them from side to side, enjoying the way the sunlight flickered through her splayed finger shadows.

The firelight flickers as people pass in front of the glowing embers. Their low voices merge with the crackle of the the sparks, the murmur of wind in the trees, and the scush of surf on the rocks of the bay.

The bear keeper's bread is heavy and dark, and his wife offers us slices of peppered ham and crumbly cheese to go with it. My mother accepts graciously, not so fast as to reveal her hunger; nor so slowly as to spurn their hospitality. I follow her lead, smiling at the children arrayed on the grass beside me, as I take the food. I look behind them to confirm the bear is himself fed and caged before I feel it is safe to eat.

In our little group there is quiet except for the

sounds of eating. After a few mouthfuls I nod and smile my gratitude and approval at my new German friends. There is an awkward silence, for this is as far as our conversation can go.

The oldest child, a boy my own age, points to himself proudly. 'Hans,' he says. He indicates in turn his brothers and sisters – Bettina, Peter, Gretchen – then points at me with a question in his face.

I put down my plate. 'Morag,' I beam. I curtsy towards him: 'Hello, Hans,' and then I work along the line of his siblings, introducing myself to each with a firm handshake. And now I turn to the bear in his cage and bow deeply, with a sweep of my arm.

'Bruin,' says the bear in a gruff voice, and I snap upright, stepping back sharply amid German giggles. The bear doesn't stir, but Calum steps out from behind his cage with a laugh. When I have recovered my composure I pretend to be angry but I cannot make it last long, and soon we are all sitting around exchanging names for each other and parts of our faces.

∿

'It's empty, isn't it?' Mrs Crawford's voice wasn't angry, just flat and empty and neutral. Abigail's flickering fingers froze in front of her. She laid her hands slowly on the desk and looked up, fearfully.

'Your homework book,' Mrs Crawford continued. 'There's nothing in it, is there?'

Abigail blushed. The book lay on her desk, its cover closed, empty indeed. *But how did she know?* Abigail thought. *Is my teacher a robot with X-ray vision? An alien in human form?*

Mrs Crawford tapped Abigail's head lightly with a ruler. 'And I'll bet there's nothing at all of my lesson in here either.'

Abigail didn't need to reply. The X-ray vision saw through her just as it did through her book.

'Where were you just now, Abigail?'

Abigail shook her head. 'I don't know.'

Mrs Crawford shook her head too. 'Oh, I think you do. You just don't want to tell us. But what bothers me is that you weren't here, in this room. You were miles away.'

Not just miles away, Abigail thought, daring Mrs Crawford to read her mind now. *Years away too.*

'To *keep* you in the room we'll move your body to the middle of it, in the hope your mind won't wander quite so easily.' She looked around, then picked out a boy in the very middle of the room. 'Andrew, will you please swap places with Abigail?'

And as Abigail gathered her things and moved dutifully towards Andrew's now-empty desk, Mrs Crawford made a mental note. *Must talk to the year head about that one*, she told herself. *She's not all there.*

Calum takes my hand and leads me on to the grass. Together with other villagers we form a line of couples. Fiddle music from the Dervaig players swells about us. The bear keeper watches and listens awhile till he has the tune, and then he too joins in. The dance is new, and I do not know the steps, but Calum guides me with his firm hand. 'Turn,' he calls. 'Turn again! Now burl!' and our arms link at the elbow as we skip and spin. I'm concentrating hard, but not so much that I cannot enjoy it. As the music continues, I learn the steps and throw myself into the dance more completely, spinning faster, skipping higher, till it seems my feet scarcely touch the ground. Calum whoops with joy and I echo him, laughing loud in between my cries from the thrill of it all.

I'm still laughing when the music stops, and I'm dizzy from the spinning, but Calum's steadying hand grips my arm till we recover our breath and stroll back to the wagon and the applause of the German children.

'What is it called, this new dance?' my mother asks Calum.

But it is Murdo who answers, stepping forward

into the light. 'It is a dance called America, about leaving home for new lands across the ocean. Will you dance it with me when they play it again?'

My mother's face darkens. 'I will not. I have little levity for dancing, nor any wish to learn the steps.'

'A shame. Then perhaps your daughter? She learns quickly, and not without enjoyment.'

My mother takes my free hand just as Calum lets the other go. 'She has danced enough for one evening.'

'Again a shame. I was just about to offer her employment. But I see you shun me still, and your daughter is so tied to your skirts she'd be of no use to me.'

'Employment?' my mother tries to empty her voice of any feeling. I know how much she needs the money, wherever it comes from.

'Indeed.' Murdo's eyes slide from my mother's face to my own. 'As a drover.'

'A drover!' I cry. 'Oh please, Mother!'

Murdo continues. 'I have a boat-load of cattle to take to Salen Fair on Monday. I'm going with Calum, but we two are not enough.' He jingles his pocket. 'A crown, I will pay. I'll even pay you now. And I'll feed her along the way.' He holds out a shining coin.

My mother does not take it. 'Very well. But only as far as Salen. And it is she you should pay.' Murdo hesitates, clearly reluctant to hand money to me. But my mother is implacable. 'And you must pay her now, as you would have paid me.'

He hands me the coin as if it were poisoned. 'Monday, dawn, at Croig pierhead,' he says, then turns on his heel and leads Calum away, giving me no chance to curtsy my gratitude or wave Calum farewell. I watch them go as I turn the coin over and over in my hand. It is more money than I have ever held. My fingers feel the heads and tails succeed each other, just as my hopes and fears rotate through my heart. To be droving at last, to be so handsomely paid for it, and to go with Calum excites me more than I can contain. But there's something about Murdo, and the way he treats my mother, and the way he gained her agreement, that I do not like.

I reach out again for my mother's hand, and slip the crown into it. There is a catch in her voice when she speaks. 'Thank you, my child. Thank you.'

Chapter 3

*A*bigail tightened her hood. The rain had stopped but the park's scattered puddles showed how heavy it had been, and now their rippled surface told of the blustery wind.

Typical, she thought. *It's sunny all week when I'm stuck in school, and now it's a Saturday morning monsoon.'*

Abigail whistled to Muppet, who ignored her, as he usually did when his walk was ending. 'Here, Fingal!' she called. The dog ignored her still, until she corrected herself. 'Here, Muppet! Come!' And he bounded up for his biscuit reward as she snapped the lead to his collar.

There was a loud burst of laughter from the bus shelter just outside the park, which fell quiet as Abigail approached. Where it had been empty earlier, at the height of the downpour, three kids her own age now slouched within its plexiglas walls. She tried not to see the mocking stares or hear the sniggered comments, but one voice rose above the others. It could not be ignored or fail to be recognised. 'Weirdo!' called Elaine. 'Don't know your own name, don't know your dog's.' And now the others joined in. 'Weirdo!' they shouted. 'You need a check-up from the neck up! Radio rental! Radio rental!'

Although I've been waiting since dawn, it is mid-morning before the last of the cattle are thrown from the boat to swim ashore, and nearly noon before Murdo joins us. I'm not sure, but I think I catch the sour reek of whisky on his breath as he strides by, counting the animals and ignoring me.

'Twenty-three,' he calls to Calum. 'Are all of them sound?'

Calum points his stick at a cow which looks to me no different from all the rest. 'This one limps.

Left foreleg. I'm not sure what's wrong.' He'd spotted it straight away, as the animals walked up the beach, but even when he pointed it out I found it hard to see.

'Aye, well,' says Murdo, after a cursory inspection, and he sets out at the head of the herd, leaving me and Calum and Fingal to follow behind it. We have to tap the animals' rumps with our sticks to keep them moving along the path, and to stop them veering off to the richer grass that grows thick on either side. But the cattle heed Fingal more than they do us or our sticks, though he never barks or growls or even bares his teeth. There's an authority in his stare, a power in his shoulders that means he never needs to.

'Dad?' He was sitting on the couch, shouting at the footballers on the TV screen. 'Dad?'

'Mmm?' He didn't look at her, but at a red-shirted

player surging past defender after defender. '*Tackle* him, will you?'

'*Dad*?'

The red marauder lost possession, and her father turned towards her. 'Yes, love?'

'What does "Radio Rental" mean?'

'I don't –' a roar from the TV whipped his head back round, and he jumped to his feet. 'Go on, son, take him on! Now cross it! No! No! No!' He groaned and sat back down, and as the TV referee whistled for a goal kick he turned back towards Abigail. 'What did you say?'

'"Radio Rental". What does it mean?'

'There used to be a high-street telly shop called that, like Dixon's or Curry's. Perhaps there still is.'

'Why would anyone shout it at – at someone else?'

'At you?'

Abigail braced herself to deliver the lie. 'Of course not. There were two boys fighting in the street. One kept yelling "Radio Rental".'

'Oh, I get it. It's rhyming slang, like the cockneys.

You know – plates of meat, feet.' More roars from the TV drew his attention back.

'So?'

'Radio Rental, mental. Mad. Bonkers. Nuts. Loony. Crackers.' The referee blew for half-time and Dad got up to head for the kitchen. He looked at her as he passed, and stopped to complete his list. 'Doolally. Weirdo.'

Abigail followed him into the kitchen, where he continued. 'They're words we all use every day, though really we shouldn't,' he said. 'They're words that hurt. They used to hurt Aunt Margaret. They still do.'

Abby pondered. More and more people were calling *her* a weirdo. *Is that what they really think of me?* she asked herself. If it wasn't true now, what about the future? What if she went the same way Aunt Margaret went? Was she destined to end up in some hospital, getting electric shocks to her brain and forced to pop pills every day?

She didn't want to follow these thoughts too far. 'Do you know any more?'

'Any more what?'

'Rhyming slang.'

'A bit. Dog and bone, phone.' A car tooted its horn and pulled into the drive. He smiled. 'Trouble and strife, wife.'

Abigail wriggled into her best cockney accent. 'So if I towld yer I called the old trouble on the dog and she went all radio on me –'

'You would mean . . .'

And now her Radio 4 newsreader voice, '. . . that I telephoned my wife and found her rather odd.'

Abigail's father laughed heartily as he added two more mugs to the tray.

'No one really talks that way, do they?' asked Abigail.

'I haven't a scooby.'

'Eh?'

'Scooby-doo. Clue.'

Abigail and her father burst into fits of giggles as Naomi and her mother came in, laden with bags. The returning shoppers looked from Abby to her father and shook their heads.

The afternoon heat hangs heavy upon cattle and drovers alike, and our pace has dropped. Fingal glides along, apparently untroubled, but every half-mile he disappears to the fresh sparkling waters of Loch Frisa on our right to re-emerge moments later, dripping wet and licking his lips. Sweating in my heavy dress, and cursing my forgetfulness in not bringing my water flask, I envy him.

Murdo still leads the herd along the path, but even he has slowed his striding. The cattle veer aside more often now and our sticks are much employed, though Fingal still trots from side to side, steering the errant beasts with his presence. Clouds of midges hang around us and cow-tails swat horseflies away, though no insects trouble the dog. *Droving is hard work*, I tell myself.

And yet . . . it makes no sense that there are three of us. Murdo marches on, though the cows are not following him – they are being driven by us, and as far as I can tell he's just idling along, lost in thought. But if this drove doesn't need three people, then why am I paid handsomely to be here?

Beside me Calum stoops to pick up a handful of pebbles. He hands two to me. 'Old McIver's cairn,' he says. 'Up ahead.'

Murdo has already passed it, unheeding – a low cone of stones on the loch side of the path, on a rise looking down to Loch Frisa. I am dry-mouthed, though whether from thirst or the knowledge that this was the spot where the water-horse leapt up from the depths of the loch and took poor McIver, dragging him back to the water where he was found floating days later, I cannot tell.

There is a clacking sound as Calum adds his stones to the cairn. I turn and do the same, then rush on. I have no wish to linger here, even in broad daylight and accompanied as I am by men and beast.

The shouts of Abby's classmates echoed back from the swimming pool's high ceiling. It was life-saving practice and the class was divided into two groups, rescued and rescuers, each assigned a bench. Abby was the last to be picked, and told she'd be a victim. She slipped her father's old pyjamas over her swimsuit and walked the length of the bench, to the last remaining seat at the far end. The pyjamas' too-long legs trailed behind her, and caught the eye of more than one fellow victim. There was nudging of elbows and a suppressed giggle as she passed. Elaine bent forward for the heavy rubber bricks they used in diving practice.

'Have you ever seen the water-horse?' I ask Calum as we near the end of the loch.

He shakes his head. 'Never. It is only seen by its victims. But I have no need to see it to know

70

that it haunts these waters, as the fairies do the land. There are so many spirits, but it is possible to know their ways and whereabouts and so to avoid them. The one-nostrilled Sith, the Glaisting, the Gruagach – I heed them all. Look.'

He rummages in his pocket and brings out a muslin purse. I do not need to open it, for a sniff tells me it is full of oatmeal. 'I carry this whenever I travel these paths to ward off the Bean Sith – the banshee – and the Tamhasgan. We may hear them tonight if we do not reach Salen by nightfall.'

I shudder.

'But fear not, Morag. My oatmeal will protect you too while you are with me. And always remember, if we are apart, that no fairy dare touch a mortal below high-water mark.'

I cannot help but smile at his belief in these superstitions. 'What if it is high tide? Must I hold the fairies at bay till the water drops? Or stick seaweed in my hair and a limpet on my nose, and pretend that high water's way above my head wherever I am?'

By way of reply Calum hurls a pebble high into the air, following it with a Gaelic curse, or perhaps a spell, spoken too fast for me to follow. It splashes right into the centre of the sun's reflection on the loch's flat surface. Golden fragments sparkle and gleam as ripples radiate across the water to dissipate in the reeds and grasses on either shore.

'There, he says. 'I have stilled the water-horse against you. And as for fairies –' he turns to face me '– I think they would take you to be one of their own before they would ever attack you.' He holds my gaze for a long silent moment, then strides off along the path before I can think of a reply.

Abby watched the other kids as they paired off in turns for the rescue. A succession of pyjama'd victims pretended to fall in at the deep end, thrashing and shrieking, while their partners played the heroic lifeguard. Abby tightened her pyjama belt and waited, wondering who would be chosen to rescue her.

Her turn came before she was ready. She was propelled forward, off the bench, and hurled into the water. She hit it hard, face down and flailing, and scarcely able to take a breath before she was submerged. She lashed out with all her limbs to wrestle her way back to the surface, but something was wrong: she didn't rise. She'd never swum in pyjamas before, but surely they couldn't be this heavy. She looked down to see, with horror, a heavy rubber diving brick wrapped in net and tied to each pyjama trouser leg. Their weight dragged her down to the black-and-white chequer-board tiles far below. She fumbled with the cord at her waist to release the pyjamas, but she'd tied and retied it so tight it wouldn't budge. Bubbles of precious air escaped her mouth as her chest spasmed, desperate for more. And the harder she thrashed the deeper she sank.

Abby's head rang and her vision closed in. Her ears began to hurt as she sank deeper. She looked down again, and suddenly realised what she had to do: find the courage to stop struggling, and let herself sink. She stretched her hands above her head, fingers spread wide, and felt for the tiles with her toes. When she touched she sank further, till she was in a deep crouch, and then, at the very end of her air, she kicked down as hard as she could against the bottom, and put all her remaining strength into powerful strokes from her arms. With this she rose enough to break the surface, where she snatched two quick breaths and looked frantically about for anything to grab. Her fingers found the lipped edge of the pool, where she hung, eyes closed and gasping. Somewhere above there were giggling children who shrank back at the approach of the furious teacher. He bent to grab Abby's wrists and hauled her up, twisting her as she rose, then lowered her to flop and gasp at the water's edge while he untied the bricks.

The lame cow's limp grows worse with time and miles, but Murdo does not wait, and he is lost to view by the time we sight Salen. We press on, our conversation sparse, and when at last we approach the hillside gathering of people and animals we are too footsore, thirsty and tired to care much where he is.

Calum spots him first, leaning on a wall and deep in conversation with two men I do not know. They do not look like Mull men to me, with their strange hats and daggers in their belts. They shrink away as we draw up, but not before I think I see a package change hands. Murdo breaks off, and steps up to greet us as if we had not been travelling together. He points to where he wants the cattle.

Once we have put the cattle to grass, and have drunk our fill of water, I feel able to look about me. We are camped in a meadow, surrounded on all sides by bare-shouldered hills. Ben Mor rises solidly to the south, and thick woodland clusters on either side of the stream to the east ahead. Beyond I glimpse rooftops, and a tall timber pier at the water's edge, where the village of Salen sits on its bay in the Sound of Mull. *This is where my work is done*, I think.

Abigail sat in the headmaster's office, changed and dry. She couldn't stop coughing, and her muscles felt bruised from her exertions. The headmaster waited for the coughs to subside.

'Try 543 5781. It's her work number,' she said, when she found the breath.

The head keyed in the numbers. 'Ah, good afternoon,' he announced. 'May I speak to Mrs Jones? Mr Arnold. Her daughter's head teacher.' He frowned. 'Yes, I'll hold.'

He put down the phone. Tinny music dribbled out across the desk for what seemed to Abigail an eternity, before a synthetic voice cut in. 'Thank you for continuing to hold. Your call is important to us and will be answered shortly –'

Abigail stiffened when the next voice came, for she knew it at once as her mother's.

Murdo lights his pipe and puffs deeply. Though I find its sweet smell sickly, I am glad of the smoke because it repels the midges that now feast on us all.

I look at the sun and test my legs for strength, wondering if I have the time and the energy to return to Dervaig tonight. I shiver at the thought of passing Loch Frisa in the dark.

Murdo smiles at me, as if in reassurance, and though his smile has something of Calum in it, there is none of Calum's warmth. 'Well done, Morag,' he says. 'A good day's work.' He hands me a slice of cheese he has carved. 'Are you up for more?'

I look up, surprised, and hesitate before I reply.

'I promised my mother I'd be back today. She will fear for me if I am not.'

'She need fear nothing.' He indicates a passing farmer. 'William there departs for Dervaig shortly. We can send word through him.'

'But what has changed to alter your plans?'

'I have learnt that we must drive these beasts ourselves now, at least as far as Oban and possibly on to Crieff. We will leave the lame one here to speed our passage.'

A glance at Calum tells me this is news to him too. I have never been offered adventure such as this. But still I hesitate.

Murdo's ready for this. 'I will see you – or rather your mother – well paid.'

I cannot refuse, and he knows it. 'I will be pleased to join you,' I tell him, and in part, at least, it is true. Calum smiles and Fingal presses against my legs, as if he too understands and wants me with him.

'Good.' Murdo smiles again and taps out his

pipe on a nearby boulder. I have never seen him smile so freely before, and he does not hold it long. 'Your first task is to build our night shelter. Calum will show you the method.'

Muppet's suppressed yelps roused Abigail from sleep. She reached down to stroke one velvet ear and soothe away his dog-dream twitches. He seemed so much heavier, sprawled across her ankles, than he ever did during the day.

Abby looked around the darkness of her bedroom, and then at the ceiling where she'd stuck luminous stars in the shapes of her favourite constellations.

She became aware of voices downstairs, talking with the urgent up-and-down of a muffled argument.

Abby eased her legs from underneath the dog and crept to the edge of her bed, where she could open the door a foot or two. The murmuring was louder but no more distinct, so she reached up for the dressing gown on the back of the door and stepped on to the landing.

In the hall below the dining-room door stood ajar, spilling yellow light and her parents' voices into the hall.

Her father sounded aggrieved. 'You mean she nearly drowned and somehow that's *her* fault?'

'He didn't say that, Dave.'

'Then tell me what he *did* say.'

'That she's getting picked on. He knows it's not right, and he's doing what he can to stop it.'

'He's not doing enough.'

'Perhaps not. He was going to wait until Parents' Evening to discuss it but today . . . today made it urgent.'

'But why Abigail?'

'Kids get picked on because they're different, Dave.'

'That's nothing new.'

'But it's the *way* she's different. They're worried about it too. You know the way she wanders off, just disappears into her head, who knows where, not paying any attention to what's going on around her.'

'Of course. She's always daydreamed.'

'Daydreaming isn't the word. It's something more than that. And she's doing it in class now. *All the time*. The teachers see it. The kids see it. *That's* why they pick on her.'

The clock by the front door continued its slow, measured ticking. Abigail counted twenty-four ticks before her father spoke again.

'Could she not just be taking time to adjust to the new school?'

'She's not handing in any homework, Dave. Who knows what she's up to when she slopes off to her room with her books? She's way behind already and there are tests coming up.'

Her father's voice came louder now. 'Tests! For God's sake, Alison! At her age?'

'She musn't start failing things, Dave. She can't afford to. We can't afford to let her.'

'So what does he suggest we do? Sit over her while she does her homework? Do it with her?'

'Well . . . yes.' Abby stiffened as her mother's steps approached the open door. Desperate to hear more, she held her breath as her mother spoke again. 'And there's something else.'

'What?'

'He wants her to see the doctor.'

The dining-room door closed firmly, muffling the rest of the conversation. Suddenly chilled, Abby crept back to her room and lay on her bed, staring at the ceiling as her mother's words reverberated around her head. *The doctor? What for? I'm not ill. There's nothing wrong with me.* She looked through the window to the stars of Orion. *Is there?*

Chapter 4

The waiting room was hushed. There were coughs and snuffles, the wail of a baby, and the creak of chairs as people leaned forward to the pile of outdated magazines on the table. But no one spoke.

Hemmed in by her parents on either side of her Abigail looked around the room, peering into the faces that gazed dully back or quickly looked away. She whiled away the wait by trying to guess what was wrong with them. *Who's getting better?* she wondered. *Who's swinging the lead? Which of us has had it? Who's the weirdo here?*

'Abigail Jones,' boomed the loudspeaker high overhead. Abby jumped, then got to her feet. She felt suddenly weak.

In the dewy cool of morning, and without the lame cow, we progress much faster along the shore road from Salen. The waters of the sound are a deep, luminous blue, unflecked by white on this windless day and reflecting the lighter blue of the high and cloudless sky. I hear a distant goose call which at first I ignore, but when it comes again, magnified and multiplied, I look up to see a great skein of greylags heading southwards in an arrow-head that points towards their winter home far over the horizon.

Their calling grows quieter as they fly away down the Sound, and once it is a distant murmur we speak again.

'Those birds winter in Africa every year,' says Calum. 'They make bigger journeys than we ever will, and they think nothing of it.'

'But they always come back, every spring.'

Calum fixes his blue eyes upon me. 'Would you ever leave?' he asks.

I am surprised at his question and answer him

carefully. 'I will be with my mother,' I tell him.

⧸

The doctor smiled as Abigail and her parents entered, but Abigail felt little warmth from it, nor any wish to smile back.

There was a silence, as if no one wanted to speak first. Abigail didn't wish to speak at all, and when the doctor looked directly at her and asked, 'What seems to be the trouble?' she did not reply.

Her mother stepped in. 'She's always been a daydreamer, doctor, but we thought nothing of it. We thought she'd grow out of it, and it didn't seem to interfere with her schooling.'

'And now?'

'Well, it's getting worse, not better, and now the school says it *is* a problem.'

'Hmm. Does it happen at home?'

'Yes. It always has – but we thought that was just Abigail. She doesn't tell us where she –'

'Is it getting worse at home?'

'I hadn't thought so. That's why it was a surprise when –'

He didn't let her finish her answers before he was ready with his next question, and his next, and his next, as he ran through his mental list. 'Does she fall over? Lose consciousness? Bite her tongue?'

Abigail shook her head each time.

'Does she go a funny colour? Make strange noises? Twitch, or jerk, or shake? Does she – ah – *wet herself*?'

'No,' said Abigail's mother. 'Nothing like that.'

Abigail blushed and looked away.

'When she comes round, does she know what's been happening around her?'

'Well, yes and no. She misses some things, and she mixes it up with whatever's gone on in her head. Sometimes she starts talking in another language.'

'Really?' The doctor raised an eyebrow, and his voice betrayed an interest he had not shown before. He sat forward. 'And what do you have to say about this, Abigail?'

Abby sat still, staring at the medical instruments scattered across the doctor's desk. She didn't speak.

'Abigail?'

◦◦

Murdo has stuck closer to us today, as if in less of a hurry, and I am aware of him nearby. I wonder if he has heard us. At a bark from Fingal he turns aside, then calls and waves. I look up, away from the shore, to see a herd of shaggy Highland cattle coming down a narrow track to join us on the road. They merge with our smaller black cattle, who heed their long sharp horns more than they do our sticks or even Fingal. The drovers seem to know Murdo and they greet us warmly.

◦◦

'Abigail?'

'Yes?'

The doctor asked you something.'

'Did he?'

'I did. I wondered where you went just now.'

'I – I got flustered, that's all. Sorry. I just don't like doctor's rooms and hospitals.'

'But what were you thinking?'

'Nothing much.'

'You mean your mind went blank?'

'Sort of.' She looked directly at him. 'I do remember wondering why I'm here when there's nothing wrong with me.'

He smiled. 'Then let's see, shall we?' He stood up, strode over to a little couch beside the wall. 'Pop up here, Abby. Let's have a look at you. Don't worry – no need to undress.'

'We're well met,' says the older drover, the one called Angus, to Murdo.

'Aye to that. Better in numbers,' says the other

– Ruaridh – to Calum. He lays his hand on a pistol at his belt. I have never seen an armed man who was not wearing a soldier's red uniform – and mother always warned me well away from them. 'Safer, y'see.'

'Safer from what?' I venture.

He turns to me. 'But surely you know?' he asks. Seeing my incomprehension, he looks at Murdo. 'Have you not told the lass?'

I stand my ground. 'Told me *what*?' I demand.

He bends low. 'The reivers!' he hisses, close in my ear. 'Cattle thieves! Brigands who'd make off with your herd and put a sword through any as stand in their way.'

When the doctor had finished shining lights in her eyes, and tapping her knees with his little silver hammer, and sticking tiny red pins in her, he sat Abigail down and spoke directly to her. 'It looks like you're right, Abby. I can't find anything wrong.'

Abby's father let out a sigh.

Her mother frowned. 'But –'

The doctor cut her off. 'I see this a lot, Mrs Jones. Let me guess, Abby. You've just started a new school, yes? And it's all a bit more serious?'

Abby nodded.

'And already they're talking about exams and tests, aren't they?'

She nodded again.

'And sometimes it's too boring, and sometimes it's too hard, and most of the time you have more interesting places to go in your head?'

Abby nodded once more, this time with a smile: he understood. 'It's like I live in black and white but I daydream in colour,' she said.

The doctor continued. 'But the trouble is the school thinks there's something wrong with someone who does what you do, Abby. Something *medically* wrong. No room for daydreams these days, you see. Even at your age.' He looked up from the folder he was scribbling in and indicated his reflex hammer, his red pins and his eye-torch. 'And sometimes, just very occasionally, they're right, and I can't know that with these simple tools.' He looked directly at Abby. 'So I'm sending you to a specialist.'

Abby's smile vanished in an instant, while relief flooded her mother's face.

'What – what will the specialist do?' her father asked.

'Ask the same questions as me. Do the same examinations as me. And then . . . there might be some scans and EEGs and things. You know, *tests*.'

The day is nearly done. We halt to make our camp at Achnacraig, on the south-western tip of Mull. Ruaridh takes me and Calum to gather driftwood for our fire, while Murdo and Angus tend the cows. Some miles away, across the slate-grey waters of the Firth of Lorne, lies the island of Kerrera, lit up by shafts of evening sunlight from a break in the clouds. Beyond it there are buildings and lights and the masts of many boats. Oban. The mainland. I straighten with my bundle of sticks, and stare across.

'The big city, eh, lassie?' teases Ruaridh.

'I have lived all my life on Mull,' I tell him. A Mull which seems smaller now.

'Not true,' says Calum. 'She's been to other islands. To Iona, to Ulva, to Gometra. I've taken her myself.'

Not far offshore a porpoise fin breaks the surface, followed closely by another and another, all heading north with the flood tide. I turn to Calum. 'Yes,' I tell him, and point across the sea. 'But *that's* the mainland. It's Glasgow and London. It is the rest of the world, all the places in our school books and in the tales of Tobermory sailors. It is Venice and Istanbul and Bombay. Places I will never see.'

'Well, lassie,' says Ruaridh, 'to me Oban's always been a fish town and a cattle port. I'll certainly see it in a new light now.'

Abigail's desk had been moved back to the window, but it seemed there was an invisible fence around it . She didn't know what Mrs Crawford – or was it the head? – had said after the incident in the swimming pool, but she felt its effect all too well. Her classmates treated her as if she wasn't there, as if her desk were empty. *As if I was a ghost*, she thought, as she turned away to the window and, beyond it, the windswept playground.

Calum and I bend for the same piece of driftwood, and our fingers meet as we grasp it. We straighten awkwardly, but neither of us lets go.

It is nearly dark, but when Lismore lighthouse flashes its beam over us there is a sadness, and a question in Calum's eyes, where I had thought to see him smile.

'You *will* leave, won't you?' he says quietly.

I do not answer at first, and he continues. 'You will go to all those places you spoke of. Maybe not soon, but you will go.'

I wait for another sweep of the lighthouse beam. 'And would you not?' I ask him.

He shakes his head. 'I am a Mull man. I will soon have land here to tend, as my father tended it before he died.'

'But it was not *his* land,' I tell him gently. 'And it will not belong to you. Those who own it will clear you and the rest of us off as soon as they earn more from sheep than they do from people. Just as they did on Ardnamurchan. Where will you go then?'

'I will face that day when it comes. But today, tonight, I have no urge to leave the place I call my home.' A cow calls in the darkness and he smiles. 'Except, of course, for droving trips.'

He turns towards our camp, where the first flames of a fire flicker upwards. He still does not let go the driftwood and neither do I. We walk side by side, carrying it between us, though it is easily light enough for one.

When Naomi left the bathroom Abigail's door stood ajar, and there was talking within, though little light emerged. Inside, in the near dark, Abigail spoke in short bursts interspersed with silence, as if she were on the phone.

She sat by her table near the window. The blind was drawn and the only light came from the harsh glare of an anglepoise lamp, which she directed towards a corner of the room. She sat close behind the light, so her face was thrown into sharp relief. Her cheekbones shone, but her eyes were unfathomable pools. When she spoke her voice was flatter than normal, and she seemed to be addressing thin air.

'Did you lose consciousness? Hmm?' she urged, then whipped the light round to illuminate her own face. Her eyes narrowed in the glare as she stretched backwards, shaking her head.

The light swung round again towards the wall, and Abby leant forwards. 'Did you twitch or shake?'

And so it continued, Abby alternately asking and answering the questions to replay her encounter with the doctor, only with herself as both fierce interrogator and hapless victim. Naomi was fascinated: this was beyond daydreaming. Part of Naomi felt that she shouldn't be watching, and should instead fetch her father – no, her mother – to see this, but instead she stayed at the door to watch. A floorboard creaked underfoot as she shifted her weight.

Now the light spun round again, but in a different direction. Its beam swung past the door. Naomi feared she had been discovered, but it swept on past, to settle on Muppet, sprawled unsuspectingly upon the bed.

'And you,' Abby continued in her interrogator's voice, though now she was addressing the dog, and moving slowly towards him as his eyes flickered awake. She carried the light before her, with a stray lock of hair falling forwards into its harsh beam. 'Do *you* grunt? Do you make strange noises?'

She bent low over him, directing the light into his increasingly worried face. 'Do you . . . have you ever . . .' Her nose nearly touched his and she lowered her voice to a raspy whisper. 'Do you . . . *wet yourself*?'

Muppet panicked, and leapt to his feet with a yelp. The lamp's beam ranged chaotically around the room as he knocked it to the floor. He crashed into the door as he made his frantic exit, and it swung wide open to frame Naomi against the landing. She and Abigail held each other's gaze for a long silent moment. 'Only messing,' said Abigail. She waited for her sister to speak, but Naomi said nothing. She didn't need to.

We cluster close around the campfire in concentric circles, defined by species and diet. There is an inner circle of three dogs gnawing on beef bones and, outside it, a ring of five people chewing on the meat the bones were once attached to. Beyond, in the outer darkness, a milling mass of cattle wander freely, grazing and chewing the cud.

It is cold tonight, for Achnacraig is low-lying and unwooded, and there are neither hills nor trees to shield us from the chill breeze. The wind digs its frigid fingers through the gaps in my thin worn clothing, so I am glad that the same wind fans the flames of our fire, spreading warmth and the salt tang of sea-soaked wood. Clusters of red and yellow sparks billow upwards in an inverse autumn. Their firefly lights flare for an instant or two against the steady background of cool star-points, then extinguish abruptly, somewhere over our heads.

The flames light up the faces of the drovers as they regale us with story after story. I cannot tell which are true, which exaggerated, and which completely made up, but I do not care, for they tell their tales so well. I take another bite of beef and listen on as Ruaridh starts another. He points at me with a haunch of beef. 'This tale's for you, lassie. Let me tell you about Marcus and his famous cattle raid. It happened not far away.'

And so we spend the evening, for it is still too early for sleep. There are more stories. There is banter, and reminiscence, and joking.

I look at Calum laughing happily beside me. When he feels my eyes upon him he turns to me and widens his smile. I suddenly know that I want to be with him as this drove continues. I want to cross to Kerrera tomorrow, and then to Oban. I want to walk with him and this herd all the way to Crieff, where these Mull men will surely turn back, but I will walk on to Falkirk, to England, to the world. I do not want this adventure, or this evening, to end.

And then Calum opens his mouth to sing. I am astonished, for I have never heard him sing before, and his voice is clear and fine. It rides up and down the slopes of a haunting Gaelic melody I know so very well.

Calum knows all the words and he pours his heart into his voice, in phrases that put me in mind of my mother. I am suddenly torn. How can I drove cattle across the country when my mother waits alone in Dervaig?

Calum stands as his song reaches its climax, and he looks straight at me. A shiver runs through me, but this is not from the cold. His final notes seem to hum in the air between us for a time after he is done, and none of us stirs. Even the cattle are still.

The moment explodes in a shower of sparks as Murdo hurls another log on to the fire, throwing out embers we have to jump back to avoid. When he turns to Calum his eyes are glittering and hard. 'You have a fine voice, lad. But you will never sing that song again while I am in your company.' He stands, then points at me. His eyes are even harder now and his face is contorted. 'And especially when I am in hers. For is she not the daughter of her mother?' And with that he picks up his bottle and strides forth into the darkness.

Abigail lay on a narrow couch in the scanning room and listened to the machinery whirring and beeping around her. She was alone in a large white windowless space – alone, that is, but for the monstrous machine that stood poised, above and behind her head, and revealed its life in little flashing lights. To her right, through a glass shield, was a darkened alcove where white-coated people pushed buttons and studied strange pictures on their TV screens. Every once in a while one or other of them looked across at her and smiled encouragement, or offered a thumbs up. They spoke to her through a loudspeaker set high in the wall, interrupting the music that was meant to make her feel more at home.

The speaker crackled again. 'OK, Abby? We'll start to move you now.' Her couch gave a little jerk, then started sliding very slowly backwards, taking her head, centimetre by centimetre, into the hole at the very centre of the machine. 'Nothing to worry about, Abby. We'll move you slowly through and take some pictures as we go. You won't feel a thing. Just try to relax.'

Relax? thought Abby. *I'm strapped into a coffin, being fed head first into a metal monster. How can I relax?*

The music stopped again. 'Just close your eyes and imagine you're somewhere else.'

Although the cattle are frightened at first, as the sea floor drops away beneath their hooves and they are forced to swim, they soon settle into a purposeful paddling and strike out across the narrowest part of the channel which separates Kerrera from the shores at Oban.

Calum and I patrol the southern margin of their route across the channel in a battered boat left on the shore for the purpose. Ruaridh and Angus, in a second boat, mark the northern limit, while Murdo and the dogs bring up the rear, ensuring the more reluctant cows do not attempt a return to the beach they've just been forced from.

There are now perhaps fifty cows in the water, lowing loudly and splashing as they swim. Some beasts show their fear in their rolling eyes and tossing heads, but most pack close together and swim directly ahead. Sitting in the stern of our boat while Calum rows, I see one cow veer away. 'Right a little,' I tell him.

'Mine or yours?' he asks innocently, and not changing course at all.

'Mine or yours what?'

'*My* right or *your* right? We're facing opposite ways.'

Now I see what the cow is making for – a low reef in the very middle of the bay, marked at either end by warning buoys. If she gets there we'll never get her off, and all our efforts will be exposed to the ridicule of watching sailors and fisherfolk. And still Calum does not turn.

'You could just say *port* or *starboard* instead,' he continues, talking more to himself than to me, or so it seems. 'But then I could ask whether you want me to *steer* to port, or *pull* harder on my port oar and so steer to starboard.'

The cow is swimming faster as she nears the reef, and my patience breaks. I stand up – a risky move in such a craft – and point with my droving stick, held out at arm's length over Calum's left shoulder. '*There!*' I yell at him. 'Go that way, and go there fast, or we shall be responsible for a castaway cow.'

And of course, with a few quick strokes, pulling harder with his right arm, the boat swings round and Calum heads off the panicky creature. We get close enough to hit the cow with our oars, but there is no need, for Calum guides her with the bow of the boat. We force her to swim in a long curving course until she rejoins the herd, just as the leading beasts reach the shore below Oban pier.

Doctor Bolton stuck the pictures under clips on the long brightly lit box on the wall, and invited Abigail to join her in studying them.

'Imagine we cut slices across your head, Alison, starting at the top and working down. And imagine that for each slice we're looking down at the inside of your head.'

'Abigail. Alison's my mum's name.'

The doctor seemed embarrassed at her mistake. 'So it is. Sorry. You see I get distracted too sometimes, eh? Where was I?'

'Slices.'

'Indeed.' She pointed to one of the first pictures. 'This is the top slice. Not much to see but your skull – this thick white thing here. And now we work down-wards.' Her hands fluttered over the lightbox like a moth's wings. 'Cerebral hemispheres, basal ganglia, cerebellum . . .

'They're quite normal.' She smiled. 'And so's the rest of the scan, just as we expected. The scan doesn't show everything, of course. Your brain's an incredibly complicated thing, and we're only just beginning to understand it.'

Abby's mother snorted. 'You're ahead of me then, doctor. I don't understand her brain at all.'

Abigail looked away from the pictures and spoke directly to the doctor. 'Does this scan show what I'm thinking?'

'No, it can't do that. It shows what your brain looks like, not what it's doing.'

'And it looks like a cauliflower,' Abigail said. 'A *hollow* cauliflower.'

Dr Bolton turned away to pick up a thick clump of fine multicoloured wires, each attached to a tiny metal button. 'Now *this* thing tells us a bit more about how your brain works. I'm going to stick these buttons all over your head, and then I'll ask you to lie as quietly as you can, with your eyes closed, for half an hour or so. Just try to think about nothing at all. You can go to sleep if you want. I'll make the room dark and quiet. We can play music or a background tape if you want. You know, birds singing, a babbling brook, the sounds of the sea – that sort of thing.'

Abby lay down on the narrow bed as the doctor started sticking the electrodes to her head. 'Can I have the sea, please? I'd like that.'

∾

Heart . . . beat. My mighty heart pumps again, sending another two-ton surge of blood around my massive body. At these depths, cruising slowly in cold Antarctic waters, it happens so seldom – just a few times each minute – that it almost takes me by surprise. It is an hour since my last breath, but I am in no hurry to surface. For I am a blue whale, the biggest creature Earth has ever seen. A hundred feet long, a hundred tonnes in weight, I make pygmies of those reptiles, the dinosaurs, which stomped clumsily about on land before they gave up the struggle against extinction. A struggle now faced by me and my kind.

Heart . . . beat. I hear whalesong, a faraway chorus of my friends, the humpbacks, as they sing across the sea their calls of loneliness and love. I hear, very faintly, a mechanical clanking, the metal throb of engines. And I hear, from time to time, the deep boom of explosions far away, and I know that men are at work again.

'Do as you will,' I tell them as I incline upwards to the surface far above. 'Do your worst. You cannot kill me, whatever weapons you wield, for I cannot be killed by anything, and I will never die. I have criss-crossed the oceans of this Earth since before men walked, and I will still be here, doing the same, when men are no more. I will outlive you, and your ships, and all your children.'

Heart . . . beat. The brightening blue light tells me the surface is close now. The engine noise comes again. The whalesong has ceased and there is a red tinge in the waters around me. 'Do your worst, you damnable monkeys. I will shrug it off. I am immortal. I cannot d–.'

DRRRRRRR! Dr Bolton rattled the little brown plastic

bottle full of tablets, then set it down abruptly on the desk. Abigail's parents exchanged glances, but all Abby could do was stare at the container. The doctor flipped open the lid and shook out a cluster of its contents. They weren't tablets but capsules, coloured pink and green, with a translucence that revealed the white powder within.

'What do you think, Abby?'

'I don't like the look of them. What are they?'

'They're the answer. The answer to your problems. Take one of these each night at bedtime and you'll be fine.'

'I'm fine now.'

'That's not what the EEG shows. Here, have a look.' She slid a large sheaf of paper on to the middle of the desk and folded it out. It bore about twenty erratically parallel lines.

Doctor Bolton waved a hand. 'These are your brainwaves. And so far they are quite normal. But then something unusual happens.' She unfolded another length of the scroll, and pointed to a strange double twitch across all twenty lines. 'See? You'd get away with one of these double spikes every hour or so. But look.' And she unfolded another page of the scroll to reveal two more double spikes. She turned the page once more, then kept turning, and there it was again. And again, and again.

'It happens a few times each minute, like a very slow pulse.'

'Like a . . . like a heartbeat?'

'Indeed. But a very slow one. And slow or fast, it shouldn't be there at all.' She slid the telltale papers aside and looked suddenly solemn. She leant forward and lowered her voice. 'You have a kind of epilepsy, Abigail.'

Abby's racing thoughts filled the silence that followed, but she could find nothing to say. She stared at the doctor as she continued.

'It's not very serious, and you will grow out of it in a few years. It's not the kind where you fall down and go blue and shake.'

'I know.' *Someone would have noticed*, she thought.

'But it does switch off your thinking. And from what

your parents say –' Her father coughed. 'From what your *mother* says, it is getting in the way of your schoolwork.' She rattled the pill bottle again. 'And these – these are the treatment.'

Abby looked round at her only ally, her father. He seemed unwilling to say anything. *I'm on my own*, she thought, and she turned back to the doctor,

'I don't need tablets,' she said. 'I'm not ill. And I don't switch *off*, I switch *over*. To a more interesting channel.'

'Abby, that's enough,' her mother scolded.

Her father spoke up at last. 'These tablets, doctor. Are they safe?'

'Of course, Mr Jones. Entirely safe.'

Abby sighed: she knew she'd lost. The doctor's smile gave her no reassurance.

❧

'Are you sure this is where he meant?' I ask Calum, as we direct the cows off the road and into a small field, overlooked by a low, dark wood.

'I'm sure of it. See the notches on the gatepost?'

I do see them, but still it doesn't feel right. I can't say why. We are on the high ground over Oban, and can see the smoke from a hundred chimneys and smell the malt from the distillery, but we can't see a single rooftop. And if we can't see other dwellings, other people, it means they can't see us. This to me seems odd, with such a valuable herd of cattle now tended by two novice drovers.

For Ruaridh, Angus and their herd have forged on ahead – *to get miles under our feet before nightfall*, as Angus put it. And Murdo, pleading business in town, has sent Calum and me to this place and told us to camp here. 'I'll be up before the fire's lit,' he told us, though what his business is, and why he needed Fingal for it, he did not say.

I survey the wood, which we'll have to enter to gather logs for our fire. It hangs over the northern edge of the field, dark and dense and scrubby, and oddly silent for the time of day. When all the cows are in, and the gate is closed behind them. Calum leads the way to the shadow of the trees. He seems oblivious to the chill that falls as we enter the wood.

I shiver – though whether from the growing cold of evening or some strange foreboding, I cannot say. I have my hands take shelter in the pockets of my dress, where I am glad to find the Molucca bean gifted me by Calum that day at Calgary. My fingers curl around its smooth surface and I smile, relieved to clutch my charm at such a time as this.

The ground between the trees is rough and I need my balance, so I take my hands from my pockets, though I still grip my fortune bean. The light in the wood is poor, but I am brought up sharp when I look down at it. For where once it had a rich chestnut sheen, my charm now bears a deathly white pallor.

I turn to Calum and hold it at arm's length.

'What does it mean that my charm changes colour?' I ask.

His eyes widen. He looks first at the bean, and then at me, and then at something behind me. His mouth widens to call out a warning.

It is too late. Brawny arms wrap round me, pinning my hands to my sides with a strength that stills all struggle. A cloud of foul breath assaults me and an alien accent hisses in my ear. 'Dinnae fight, lassie, for we have ye.'

'Reivers!' I yell. I kick hard backwards and connect with his shin. There is a grunt, and I am hurled face-down to the ground. Before I can move a huge weight presses down on my back, pinning me there. I scream, but only once, for a stinking gag is stuffed into my mouth. I kick and strike out desperately, till my hands are tied tight behind me and the weight moves down to my legs.

I look around for Calum, and see him engaged in a furious struggle with another man who I think I have seen before. Calum's head is bloodied and the man much bigger, but Calum swings at him with a broken branch and forces him to retreat.

'Morag!' calls Calum. 'Are you hurt?'

I cannot reply.

'We dinnae want tae hurt ye, boy,' says the man as he backs off, 'but if we have tae, we will. So go easy, eh?'

Calum snarls. 'You will not have these cattle.' The man just laughs. Calum swings again, and this time he connects. A weal opens on the man's cheek and blood spills down. He's not laughing now. 'Oh, we've not come for cattle, boy,' he says with menace.

Suddenly the weight pressing me down is gone as he rises to the aid of his partner. As the two of them close in on Calum I scramble to my feet and run for the road and whatever help I can summon.

I'm through a gap in the wall and racing over the field, hampered by my skirts and the binding of my hands and the gag that fills my mouth.

The cows part before me and I see the gate. The sound of pursuit tells me I have a start, but it may not be enough. I launch myself at the gate, trying to get enough height to roll over the top, but I hit it hard, so I am winded and stuck half over.

The pain in my ribs is dreadful, but I somehow heave my legs over and fall in a heap on the other side. I try again to get to my feet, but a stick is thrust into my chest and threatens to skewer me to the ground.

My captor looks down, breathless, angry and triumphant. 'Like I said, lassie. Dinnae fight, for we have you. And it is you, and not these beasts, that we have come for.'

Chapter 5

There is a heaviness in my head, and a churning in my stomach when I rouse. My hands and feet are bound and I am blind-folded but the gag is gone, replaced by a scarf tied tight across my mouth. The smell of hay, the bucking, swaying movement, and the clip of horses' hooves tell me I am laid in a farm cart, and it is on the move. I listen longer, and hear low talk above me from the cart's driving seat.

'I wonder what he wants her for?' asks one.

'Whatever it is he must tame her first. She fought like a cat.'

'Aye, and I bear the scratches to prove it.'

'But these twenty guineas will heal all our wounds.' There is the jingle of a coin purse. They laugh, and their talk turns to other matters.

My blindfold is thin, and an edge of light shows beneath it. I rub my head against the cart's boards till the edge widens as the blindfold rides up and I can see about me.

I am surrounded by bales of hay and therefore shielded from the view of anyone else on the road. Above me a midday sun dapples light through overhanging branches, whose leaves have begun to turn. Between them I see mountains, gentler and more wooded than those of Mull. I judge from the sun that we are travelling south-east. There is no sign of Calum: I am alone.

I look to my cackling captors, and now that I have time to study them and their clothing I am able to work out why they seem familiar. Back on Mull, after our long hot walk with the cattle, it was these same two men who had been talking to Murdo at Salen and who had slunk away at our approach. It could only mean one thing: this was Murdo's doing. He beguiled me away from my mother, took me to the mainland, and set these men upon his own nephew in order to kidnap me. Though I can find no reason why, I know he must have plotted it from the outset, back in Dervaig. A rush of fury surges through my body and clamps my hands into fists, but my bindings are tight and my anger has no outlet, at least for the moment.

An hour or two later I hear the clip-clop of an approaching cart and draw my feet up beneath me, ready to rise in search of rescue. I roll forward, steady myself, and wait till I hear the horses' breathing and the other driver calling a greeting. I push down hard with my heels and raise my battered body up to the level of the bales.

I am brought up short by a rope around my waist. It digs into my ribs and I slump back down on to the boards to which I am tethered, as helpless as any farm animal led to slaughter.

The man who caught me waits till the other cart is gone, then looks down on me with a scowl.

'There will be no rescue and no escape, lassie, ye ken?'

I glare at him, hating every detail of his ugly face.

He whistles. 'And now I must blindfold you again. For if looks could kill, I'd be a corpse.' He reties the blindfold tighter than before, then removes the scarf from my mouth.

'Calum!' I shout. 'What have you done with him?' And I scream for help as loud as I can, raising flocks of startled rooks from the overhanging trees.

A bitter liquid is forced into my mouth and the scarf retied before I can spit it out. I feel a warm burning down my throat as I swallow it.

'There is none but crows here to hear ye, lassie. But ye require us to quiet ye doon again.'

He goes on but I hardly hear him, for my world is closing in and the heaviness in my head increases until I cannot hold it up. I slump to the boards, where all I am aware of is darkness, the shaking of the cart and the smell of stale hay.

'Not hungry, Abby?'

'I feel a bit sick.' Abigail pushed aside her almost untouched plate and got up from her chair. As she stood she bumped the table, slopping tea from Dad's mug and juice from Naomi's glass.

'Hey!' Naomi protested. 'That's the second time today. Do you have to be so clumsy?'

'Sorry,' said Abby flatly.

Her father frowned. 'What are you up to this afternoon, Abby?'

'Don't know. I might watch telly.' She slumped into the armchair.

'What's on?' he persisted.

'Don't know.'

'Muppet could do with a walk.'

'Maybe Naomi could do it for once.'

'I'm busy. *I've* got a life,' Naomi replied swiftly, and she too left the table.

Her mother turned in her chair. 'Abby, these things –

the sickness, the tiredness, the clumsiness – they'll pass soon. The doctor told us you get side effects for the first few days, and then they go away. Soon you won't notice you're taking the tablets at all.'

'Except when I take them.'

Her father finished mopping up his tea. When he spoke he sounded earnest and concerned. 'Abby, if you're not feeling better by Monday I want you tell me, OK?'

'OK,' she sighed. Not that it would make much difference.

When I come to next there is movement again, but of a different sort. Where before I shook and rattled on a rutted road, now I glide at speed along smooth rails. Where there were hooves of a horse, now there is the rhythmic puffing and throb of a man-made engine. And in place of the open sky above my head, there is a rain-streaked, soot-pocked window beside it.

My blindfold has vanished and I am free to look through the window. We speed past building after building, packed in more tightly than seabird nests on the cliffs of Mull. Clouds of smoke and steam whirl in our wake. The air outside looks thick and cloying, while here within it is stale and overheated and stinks of tobacco. Although I have never before seen either I find myself now on a train, passing through a city.

I turn and draw my gaze away from the outside world. I am enclosed in a small compartment, hemmed in against the window by a stern woman dressed in dark city clothes. A man in uniform stands in the doorway to the compartment. He is looking at me.

When he speaks there is at first a strange disconnection between the movement of his mouth and the sounds that come out. I shake my head and force myself to concentrate to bring him back into focus.

'No, madam,' he says. 'She don't look well at all.' I have heard his accent before, but only in the mouths of English soldiers.

The woman's voice is hard and clear but difficult to place. There is some Scots within it, but it is only faint. 'So my employer – her guardian – is bringing her from the cold damp Highlands to the warmth and good food of his own London home, so that she may recover under his roof, tended by the best doctors.'

'Very generous of him, madam.'

'Indeed it is.' She doesn't seem pleased to say it, and she looks back at me as she continues. 'Some say he is too generous. You may know of him. Colonel Williams, recently returned from India.'

'Williams of Amritsar?'

'The very one. Here. I have a letter from him.'

She thrusts a parchment at the hapless official, whose schooling has not taken him past the stage of reading aloud. '*To whom it may concern*,' he pronounces, '*please grant safe passage to my ward, as she travels south to her new home with me. She is very ill —'*

At this outrageous lie I try to rise, but my legs will not bear me. I try to speak, but my words spill out in a jumbled mix of English and Gaelic and my lolling tongue makes it hard for even me to make them out. 'I'm un-ill. I'm taken by reivers,' I burble.

The woman's bony hand thrusts me back into the seat with a surprising strength. She produces a bottle from her bag. 'Some water, miss?' she coos, though she does not wait for an answer. The cool liquid is welcome enough as she urges it between my lips, but I detect a faint trace of the same bitter substance my captors used to rob me of consciousness. I lack the strength to protest.

The man reads on, '— *she is very ill, and may at times speak strangely. She needs treatment, and privacy, though there is no risk of contagion. Colonel Henry Williams, MC and Bar.'*

The man returns the letter to the woman. It's

obvious he doesn't want to get too close to me.

'We'd value a compartment to ourselves all the way to London, if it is possible,' the woman says. I cannot say if she is asking or telling him.

He doffs his cap. Whichever way she'd meant it, he took it as an order. 'Of course, madam,' he says. 'I'll ensure it.'

Miss Crawford guided Abigail to her desk, watched by the other pupils and the head teacher, who stood at the front. When Abby was seated Miss Crawford went to stand beside him.

'Good morning, children,' she said.

'Good morning, Miss Crawford,' they chorused in reply.

Abigail joined in listlessly. 'Good morning, Mr Reynolds.'

The head stepped forwards to speak. 'Abigail's not been very well recently. That's why she's been away a lot the last few weeks. I'm very glad to know she's getting better, with the help of the doctors, and especially glad to see her back here with us today. Miss Crawford and I would like you to join us in welcoming her back.'

A classroom full of heads nodded. Even Elaine was shocked to see Abigail so pale and drawn.

'Good,' declared the head, and led the class in clapping Abigail to her desk. Abigail blushed and didn't know where to look.

Miss Crawford saw Mr Reynolds out, and when she returned she noted Abigail's attention already wandering off to the window – though it didn't linger there long. Heavy rain made it hard to see out. Abigail bent over her textbook, not feeling Miss Crawford's approving eyes upon her, and instead turned her attention inwards, in search of the windows inside her head. She'd always taken for granted the way they would open out on to other worlds more exciting, more vivid, more real somehow, than this dull dead one. It would simply happen, without effort or striving on her part. *Maybe that's it*, she thought. *Maybe I just have to try harder. Maybe now I have to* make *it happen*.

She thought for a while, then brought her hand up to cover her nose and mouth like a mask, and breathed in through her fingers so her breath sounded loud and close and hissing.

It is very dark here, so deep below the surface, and the powerful lights on my diving helmet illuminate only a small area in front of me. Strange fish drift into my view and scuttle away in alarm as my bubbles rise past their flanks.

'Turn to your left,' says the tinny voice in my earpiece as I am guided by my technical crew in our boat far above. They monitor me, my air supply, and my course towards our target: the last undiscovered wreck from the Spanish Armada. The one with all the gold.

'It should be right in front of you now.'

Still I see nothing.

'But you haven't got long. Your air's getting low and your CO_2's rising.'

I swim forwards slowly, but the current is stronger than I expected and the effort makes me breathless. There is a ringing in my ears and a prickle in my fingertips. Warning signs, I know, but my thinking has slowed and I forget what they warn of.

'That's enough now,' someone says, very far away. 'Time to come up.'

Who are they talking to? I wonder dumbly as I swim on.

'Can you hear me?' someone pleads very faintly. 'Do you read me?'

❧

'Can you hear me, Abigail?' said Miss Crawford. 'I asked if you would read for us. Page thirty-four.'

Abby flicked through the pages. She sighed and bent to the book.

'"London was by this time not just the capital of

129

Britain,"' she read, '"but the hub of the biggest empire the world has seen."'

❧

I am no longer drugged, for my weakness, hunger and disorientation forestall any attempts at escape though my severely dressed companion, whose name I still do not know, keeps close yet.

Our train pulls into an enormous barn-like structure, a building vast enough to enclose the biggest castle on Mull. We come at last to a halt. The engine rumble stops and there is a hiss of steam. People bustle bags and boxes off the train and on to the crowded platform alongside, but my keeper does not move. I turn to her, and squeeze all my concentration into my first coherent words for two days. 'Where are you taking me?' I ask her.

'You will see your new home soon enough.'

'But –'

She cuts me off as the porter comes to the

compartment door. He reaches up for her bags from the overhead racks, and when he leaves I follow him with my eyes. Now that the platform crowd has thinned I see a magnificent coach standing to one side, with two black horses munching oats from their nosebags.

My keeper is aware of my gaze. She turns to me. 'Our carriage, Elisabeth.'

'My name is –'

'Elisabeth. You have been reborn into a new life, where you will bear a new name. Elisabeth is what you are called and what you will answer to. My name is Miss Wallace. You will call me Ma'am. I run your guardian's household.'

'Guardian?' I venture. 'My mother –'

'– is replaced in the role of parent, and you will be the better for it.'

Inwardly I seethe, being robbed of both my mother and my name, but I resolve to stay calm until my strength is renewed. The short walk from the train to the coach drains all energy from my legs, and I need to be lifted bodily into my seat.

I will wait, I tell myself, as a porter loads me into the coach. *I will watch, and listen, and learn. I will bide my time till I am ready, and then, at the first opportunity, I will break free, and find my way north.*

From the carriage windows London is laid out before me. There are buildings vaster and more imposing than ever I guessed, and my eyes are drawn upwards everywhere I look. Domes glow marble-white, copper-green and burnished gold, and flag-flapping church towers pierce the high blue sky. We pass under elaborate archways, past heroic bronze statues, across grand squares, and along avenues of noble trees. Oban had felt huge to me, at least in comparison with my home hamlet of Dervaig, but this London has a scale impossible to contemplate. I lower my gaze.

Down at ground level coaches and carriages of all kinds ply along roads as wide as Mull meadows, and along their edges people pass in throngs. Some are dressed lavishly, the women in silks and bonnets and the men in frock coats and top hats; some are in work clothes or uniforms, but most dress as meanly as the poorest people of Mull. None will meet my eye. The smart ones look away with a haughty disdain, while the poor slide their gaze sideways. I see not a single smile. On Mull, when people pass on a road, there is always a greeting, no matter who they might be.

I close my eyes, but now my other senses are overwhelmed. The noise is not as loud as the Atlantic breakers on Calgary beach, but it assaults the ears with an insistent buzz. The smell in the air is not as powerful as seabird guano, or drying kelp, or burning heather, but it repels as those smells do not, for it is the smell of people by the million. And there is water here, though it is not the sparkling ribbon of the Sound of Mull but the tired and sludgy Thames, a sickly clotted brown swirl gasping its way under clanking bridges to the sea.

London, I think, *How can I – how can* anyone –

live here? Short days ago I told Calum I wanted to leave Mull – for this!

The carriage halts outside yet another imposing building, a tall but narrow house set back from a quiet crescent-shaped street and standing alone in its high-walled grounds. It is our destination.

۞

Muppet scampered back towards Abby, a large stick in his mouth. Leaves scattered in his wake as he swept round and came to a halt before her. He didn't so much drop the stick as hurl it at her feet, then looked up at her, half insistent, half pleading.

It was as if Abigail hadn't seen him at all. She side-stepped off the path and walked slowly on, oblivious both to her dog and the underfoot leaf-shuffle she'd enjoyed every other autumn.

Muppet watched her awhile, then grabbed the stick and raced ahead of her again. A second time he dropped the stick before her, and a second time she ignored him and walked on. He tried once more, but this time spun round right in front of her and dropped the stick on her toes.

Abigail moved the stick aside with her foot and trudged on her way. This time Muppet gave up, and sat with the stick between his forepaws. His tail-wagging slowed as the distance grew between them. Eventually it stopped altogether, and he looked around for someone else to play with.

'Check the dog,' said Elaine to her friends as they slouched on a nearby park bench. 'Even he thinks she's boring.'

'It was better when she was weird,' another girl replied as Muppet came over and presented the stick.

'Yeah. More room to take the mickey.'

'You can't tease someone that boring.'

'Oh, I don't know.' Elaine got up from the bench. She held her arms straight out in front of her and walked lurchily dead ahead towards Muppet, with stiff knees and a fixed unseeing gaze. A strange noise emerged from her throat, a kind of dull lowing.

'Zzzzzzzooooooooommmmmmmmbbiiiiieeeeeeessss,' she moaned.

Muppet backed off, hackles rising on his shoulders and a growl growing in his chest. The girls sniggered to show how little they feared him, and one by one joined Elaine in her aimless zombie dance. Muppet yelped and fled, his tail between his galloping legs.

At the far end of the park Abigail looked round to see a frightened dog hurtling towards her and a pack of zombies stumbling over the bench amid shrieks of cruel laughter. She turned away again and walked on.

I wake in a bed softer and warmer and wider than any I have ever known. The linen is clean and crisply starched, and where I used to lie under a worn sheepskin, here I have a feather-filled cover. I enjoy the unaccustomed luxury while I look around to get my bearings. My head is clear at last and I can take in the large airy room, with sun streaming through autumnal trees to strike the window in angled shafts. There is a dressing table, and a bookshelf, and a wardrobe. Hanging on the outside of it is a dress of a kind I have rarely seen and never worn. It is of white cotton, with dark-green silk edging and an embroidered bodice. It is obviously meant for me.

I slip out of bed, almost tripping on the fine new shoes laid out at my feet. They are the kind that would fall apart on contact with mud or salt water, and are meant instead for indoor wear in city rooms. I slip them on, astonished at their lightness, and I step to the window. Far away, but still within the house, I hear bells and the raking out of last night's fires. I open the window, and in pour the distant sounds of the city: horses' hooves and the creak of cartwheels, the toot of a train whistle, the echoing blast from a steamer on the river. From close at hand birdsong ripples up to fill the gaps in the city noise. I do not recognise any of their calls. There are no gulls, nor greylags nor eider ducks, but the trills and chirps are pretty enough for creatures of the town.

There is a knock on the door, but before I answer it swings open and Miss Wallace sweeps in, bearing a tray. There is a pot of steaming tea and the warm smell of toast. Dabs of butter rise in a pile from a delicate china plate, and a rich red jam fills a matching china bowl. I am suddenly hungry.

'Breakfast, child,' she says, setting down the tray. 'When you have eaten you will wash, and dress, and await my return. Colonel Williams has summoned you.'

Abigail's year, and the year above, were gathered in the school gym. Miss Rogers, the drama teacher, and Mr Buchan, from the music department, stood on the stage, and called for quiet.

The noise simmered down and Miss Rogers

stepped forwards. Mr Buchan played two loud dramatic chords on the piano, and an expectant silence finally settled as the notes died away. Miss Rogers was slightly built, but she needed no microphone to fill the hall with her voice. Mr Buchan looked on admiringly as she readied herself to speak.

'I'm sure you're all wondering what the play will be this year,' she began. 'It's a marvellous modern musical.' She ignored the groans. 'You'll know some of he songs already. There are some major roles, and we'll be holding auditions for anyone who's interested. We'll have a big chorus for anyone who wants to be in it – no tests, no auditions. All you need is some enthusiasm. And for anyone who doesn't like being onstage there's make-up, lighting, sound, costumes, front of house. There's something for everyone.'

There was a hubbub of conversation until Miss Rogers spoke again. 'You don't have to make your minds up yet, but in order to find out more, I want you to divide up . . . Solo roles, under the far basketball hoop.' A clutch of eager stars jumped to their feet and ran the length of the hall. 'Chorus people, up here on stage. Technical staff, over by the side wall.'

Nearly everyone moved off, but Abby felt no urge to join any of the groups. She looked around and saw three or four other kids who'd stayed put like her. She recognised them. *Every class has its weirdo*, Naomi had said. *Don't be the weirdo in yours*.

Miss Crawford stepped forwards. 'Staying here's not an option, Abby. Why not join the chorus?'

Abigail looked at her. 'I can't sing,' she said simply.

Miss Crawford smiled. 'That doesn't stop the others. Half of them are tone-deaf. And there's plenty of time for practice. If you're really worried you can just mouth the words – you know, mime it. No one will know.'

And with that she led Abby to the back of the unruly queue that snaked up the stage steps.

Ahead of me Miss Wallace knocks on the heavy oak door. After a pause, a deep voice commands us to enter. Miss Wallace pushes the door open and leads me through, stepping aside once we are within.

The room is large, high-ceilinged, and richly furnished. Portraits and large tapestries adorn the walls, and above the black marble mantelpiece are the mounted antlers of a creature unlike any I have seen on Mull. Deep leather armchairs flank the fireplace, where a newly built fire flickers into life. Nearby are low tables laden with ornaments – a copper duck, a painted statue, an antique pistol. Before the fire is stretched out the orange-and-black striped skin of an enormous tiger, whose stuffed head bares gleaming fangs at me.

And on the skin stands Colonel Williams. He is tall and broad-shouldered, and carries himself with the air of a man who has served a lifetime in the Army, though in place of uniform he now wears city clothes.

'We meet at last,' he says. He dismisses Miss

Wallace with a wave of his hand, then steps forwards and clamps my shoulders in a powerful grip. 'Now let me look at you.'

And while he does, I study him in return. I notice a jagged scar on the back of one hand, which zigzags over his wrist to disappear under his cuff. His starched white collar sets off a deep tan. His hair is black, though greying at the temples, and he sports a bushy moustache which hides his mouth. Whatever is going through his mind I cannot tell, for his is a face which gives nothing away. His gaze bores into me, stilling my questions before I give them voice.

He straightens, his inspection done. 'A fine girl.'

His presumption emboldens me to speak. 'My mother –'

'– knows you are safe and well and here with me. I have seen to it. For I am your . . . guardian. Now that I have left the Army and returned from India, I thought it time to take a keener interest in your welfare.' He takes a cigar from his breast pocket and a match from a silver box on the mantelpiece.

'She never spoke to me of a guardian,' I venture.

'No?' The match flares, and he draws on the cigar. Once lit he puffs out clouds of evil-smelling smoke, then looks to me again. 'Perhaps she sought to protect you. To live your life of miserable poverty was hard, I'm sure.' He gestures at the opulence all around us with the cigar. 'And so much harder if you knew this could be your home instead.'

I bristle at this. 'My home is on Mull, with my mother.'

He snuffs the still-flaring match with his bare fingers. 'You are here to further your education in the ways of society. You will come to enjoy London and all it offers.' He hurls the smouldering match into the fire and bends towards me, lowering his voice. 'But if, in your ignorance, you seek to return to Mull, you will have made a mistake.' Another cloud of smoke engulfs me, and

I feel sick. 'For I have already arranged to refurbish your cottage, ready for its next tenant.'

He straightens and studies the shock and the puzzlement my face must have shown. 'Evictions are nearing Dervaig, and you and your mother are marked out as among the first to go if you displease me.'

Though we all feared the Clearances would come to Mull in time, this is the first I have heard they are so close. Nowhere in the Highlands was safe from greedy landlords who would turn tenants out from their ancestral homes and give their land over to sheep. Those they displace camp where they can or wander in search of new homes, a journey that takes most of them over the sea to America, to Canada, to Newfoundland. And here is this man, threatening such a fate for me and my mother if I do not obey him. Heat rises in my cheeks.

He continues. 'Heed me, do my bidding, stay here as my ward as long as I wish it – and I will ensure your mother has a comfortable home and a stipend to boot. She will never go hungry again. You may write to her – but only through me.' And now he comes close, to hold me in his fierce gaze again. 'But if you chafe at your new life, and find yourself drawn northward, think of this: your mother will find herself evicted, and her possessions burned, long before you ever reach Mull.'

The terrible truth bears down upon me: my poor mother is now a hostage, and he dangles the threat of Clearance over her to ensure my compliance with whatever he has planned for me.

My eyes must show my anger, for he continues. 'I have the means – and, believe me, I have the will – to do this, however much it pains me to think of that woman reduced still further to penury, and to camping in Dervaig churchyard. Surely it must pain you too, Elisabeth.'

He uses my hated new name as a test. If I answer to it, he knows he has me, if only for today. But how can I refuse it, knowing the power he wields? I am confused into silence by this and other questions. *How does he know my mother? Why has she not spoken of him? What does he want with me?*

'Calum,' I ask eventually. 'What happened to Calum?'

'Calum? Ah yes, the young man who fought so hard to protect you. I have him marked for one of the Highland regiments in a year or two. Rest assured, he is well.' He throws the unfinished cigar into the flames. 'And now, shall I show you round your new home?'

It is not a question, so I do not answer, but follow him in silence as he marches towards the door.

Abigail hummed as she cleaned her teeth. It was a tuneless humming, made more so by the droning buzz of her electric toothbrush. Only she could pick out any kind of melody, and only she knew it was the song she hated most from the school play. She'd been singing it, along with the rest of the chorus, for weeks now, and she couldn't get it out of her head.

Her free hand rummaged in the cabinet above the sink and found the little plastic bottle she was looking for. She flipped it open to reveal the cluster of green and pink capsules nesting within. Switching off the toothbrush, she ceased her humming and shook two capsules into the palm of her hand. Only then did she hear the ghastly moans on the landing.

She looked up to see Naomi lurch stiff-legged into the bathroom, her arms held straight before her and a stupid expression on her face. When she was sure she'd been seen, Naomi dropped her arms to her sides and came to a halt. 'Oh, sorry,' she said with a smirk. 'Don't know what came over me. Have you finished?'

Abigail contemplated her sister. 'What was all that about?'

Naomi edged her aside. 'All what?'

'That zombie business. They do it all the time at school. I shouldn't have to put up with it here.'

Naomi shrugged. 'You were singing your zombie music. I just had to join in.'

'I hate that stupid song as much as you do. It's driving me nuts.'

Naomi turned and looked directly at her. 'No, Abby. You were nuts before. I saw you with Muppet, remember? It's only those pills that stop you freaking out completely, like Aunt Margaret. But now, with the pills – now you're just a zombie.'

Try as she might to hide it, enough of Abigail's hurt must have shown on her face, because when Naomi spoke again her voice had softened. 'Not much of a choice, is it? Go mental or stay a zombie.'

Abby watched her leave, then closed the bathroom door. The capsules grew sticky in her hand as she studied her reflection in the mirror. She looked down at the pill bottle, and then, a decision reached, she replaced the capsules in the bottle, closed the top, and returned it to the shelf. When she closed the mirrored door to the cabinet her reflection swung back to face her again, but with a different look in her eyes.

There was a knock at the door. 'All right, Abby?' her mother called.

'Yes,' Abigail replied firmly. 'I've finished.'

All but the most stubborn leaves have left the trees of the orchard. I watch from my window, in the early twilight of November, as the gardener sweeps them from the grass and piles them into his barrow.

I am dressed formally in a dark gown and slippers and my hair is braided, for today, two months after my arrival in London, I am to be Presented. After two months of coaching in how to speak, and move, and curtsy, Miss Wallace has told the Colonel I am ready, and he has invited a houseful of guests before whom he plans to parade me. His Highland ward, he calls me, as if I am a kind of performing animal, captured in the remote wilderness and brought to town to entertain the gentry. I sympathise with the bear that danced for us at Dervaig as I wait for the crowds to arrive.

⚬

Abigail waited in the wings with the rest of the chorus, watching but not joining in as their nervous energy had them adjusting costumes, checking each other's make-up, and peering through the gaps in the curtains. They'd been rehearsing hard for months for this moment, but now, as the first-night audience filed in to take their seats, none of them felt ready. Abby started humming. She hated the way this song, with its dippy melody and cheesy lyrics, stuck in her head.

But now, minutes before she was due to sing it, along with the rest of the chorus, to an audience of families she suddenly doubted herself. How did that stupid melody go? What were those words again?

The lights in the hall went down, and the audience hushed. Abigail's mouth went dry.

⚬

I pace round my room, counting the arrivals in the hall below, listening to the rising hubbub of visitors' voices, and waiting for the knock at my door. I am eager for my ordeal to begin, that it may be over the sooner.

But Miss Wallace does not knock: she sweeps directly in and throws me a quick smile. She holds out her hand. 'Come, Elisabeth,' she commands. 'It is time.'

And as she draws me on the long walk to the hall, she reminds me of all she has instilled in me since my arrival in London. 'Now remember: speak only when spoken to, smile and curtsy, and soften the rough edges of your speech. You will do well to tell the Colonel's guests how much you value what he has done for you.'

At the top of the staircase she turns to look directly at me. 'And on no account will you speak of Mull or your mother, if ever you wish to see them again.'

I look hard into her face, trying to fathom her

out. She's a Scot, like me, though it hardly shows now. She fills every waking hour running the household, doing the Colonel's bidding. She has no other life. I know nothing of her past. Was she plucked, like me, from a Highland home by a London lord? Why did she not rebel?

I find no answer in her eyes, and resolve to give nothing away in mine. 'I understand,' I tell her meekly, and descend the first step.

After such a nervous wait, Abigail was relieved the performance had at last begun. She stood amid the chorus at the left of the stage, glad of the anonymity of numbers, and watched the soloists prance and sing in front of her. Her costume felt itchy and ridiculous, and she fiddled awkwardly with her long shepherd's stick.

The rest of the chorus peered eagerly past the dazzling footlights and into the audience, looking out for family, so they'd know who to sing to when the moment came. Abby hadn't shared their eagerness, at least until now, but as the music plinky-plonked its way towards their first song, and she readied her voice, something stirred within her – something she hadn't felt for months, since the start of Tablet Time. It was if long-set clouds were suddenly clearing overhead, as if a murky window had swung abruptly open.

Abigail stepped forwards to the edge of the stage. The musicians faltered and exchanged puzzled glances. Abigail took a deep breath.

There are more people gathered than I expected, and they are dressed in their full finery as if this is a special occasion on their social calendar – and it is. Who would refuse an invitation from Colonel Williams?

The women sit in little groups, twittering like sparrows of fashion and gossip, while the men stand and rumble on about share prices and politics and war. All heads turn, and most chatter stops, as Miss Wallace leads me into the room and towards Colonel Williams, resplendent on his tiger-skin at the mantelpiece.

The guests part before us as we pass through the room towards him, and when I too am standing on the tiger Miss Wallace guides me in a half-turn till I face the room and the gathered crowd. Williams steps up behind me and lays his powerful hands on my shoulders. The room goes quiet.

'Ladies and gentlemen, friends and colleagues,' he booms confidently. 'Valuing your company as I do, I need no occasion to share it; but we are gathered here on the introduction of this young lady to London life and the best of London society. She is my Highland ward, whom I first encountered when I was garrisoned in that wild corner of our great country.' His hands grip me tightly, forestalling the turn he knows I would make on hearing that we have met before: it is the first I know of it. If it is not a lie.

'Now that she is nearly grown and I am free, after a lifetime of duty, to devote myself to her development, I have brought her here that she might learn. I hope you will take her to your hearts as much as I have to mine' – again the tightening of the hands. 'Allow me to present Elisabeth Williams.'

A polite murmur of applause ripples around the room, but I do not hear it above the blood pounding hotly in my ears. Not only has he stolen my own name, now he forces on me his own. I will not – I cannot – endure it.

He bends forwards and whispers in my ear, smiling all the while as if he is murmuring encouragement. 'Curtsy and smile,' he demands. 'And remember it is November, and cold in Dervaig with no roof over your head.'

When he senses that I have swallowed my anger he relaxes his grip and steers me towards a group of seated women who smile at me stiffly.

'And how do you like London?' the oldest among them asks.

I glance at the Colonel. He watches, but not too closely. ''Tis not so large as Mull,' I say hesitantly. 'Nor so mountainous, nor so ringed about with bright water.'

'Oh but we have the Thames,' she gushes back.

'And Highgate Hill,' another one titters.

'But what of London – the buildings, the people?' a third pushes the question back at me.

I ponder. 'The buildings are grand and the people are many. But when I think of home it is not buildings or people that first come to mind; it is the sea, and the hills, and the creatures that share them with us.'

'Home? But surely this is your home now, child?'

Williams has edged closer to listen. I speak up. 'The Colonel has generously provided for me, but as to home –'

Miss Wallace grasps my wrist and draws me away. 'As to home, you could wish for none finer, eh? Now, child, let me introduce you to Lady Lewisham.'

And as she drags me across the room she hisses in my ear, 'Be very, very careful.' And I am thrust before another gaggle of women, though these remind me less of sparrows than a parliament of crows with their shiny black gowns and flinty hard eyes and carrion-coated beaks. At the centre of the group is a wrinkled old woman. She looks at me as if working out which of my eyes to peck out first.

Miss Wallace curtsies. 'Lady Lewisham, may I present Colonel Williams' ward?'

The crow beak opens. Cake crumbs clog her yellowed teeth and stick to her bloodless lips. 'Ah yes.' She stretches to me, unleashing a cloud of foul city breath no amount of perfume can hide. 'And how do you like London, Elisabeth?'

I can dam it up no longer, however much I should dissemble for the sake of my mother. The truth wells up within me, like a mountain spring after rain.

'London is an impressive city,' I tell the crow queen. 'But it is not, and will never be, my home. And Elisabeth is a pretty name for an English girl but it is not, and will never be, mine.' I look around the little group, from one shocked face to another, and then, over Lady Lewisham's shoulder, I fix the Colonel in a steely gaze. 'Call me Morag. Morag McGregor from Mull.'

Abigail blinked in the footlights' glare and the shocked silence of the audience. The music had stopped, the singing had ceased, and cast, chorus and musicians now looked around, paralysed with uncertainty.

Someone laughed, and a murmur went round the audience, raising other laughs and an embarrassed shifting of chairs. Mr Buchan started up the piano again, and signalled the musicians and the chorus to follow him. Miss Rogers dashed from the wings, grabbed Abigail and dragged her offstage.

As she was pulled away, Abigail heard the chorus behind her lurch raggedly into the song she had come to hate. Her parents appeared moments later.

'What on earth –' said her anxious father.

'What happened, Abby?' demanded her mother angrily. 'And who is Morag McGregor?'

❧

Miss Wallace drags me sharply towards the door, pursued by tuttings and mutters of disapproval. The Colonel follows us out of the room.

'Miss Wallace!' he booms down the corridor. She stops, and we turn to face his wrath as he marches up. 'What happened?' he demands.

For once Miss Wallace is uncertain. 'She . . . she . . .'

'WELL?' he roars.

'I was wrong. She is not yet tamed, Colonel Williams, and I fear she may never be. You have taken the child out of Mull, Colonel, but you

159

cannot take Mull out of her.'

He glares at me fiercely. I glare back. He stoops and brings his face close to mine. 'I have met wilder creatures than you, my dear, and none ever defeated me. I have tamed tigers. I have fought lions. I will tame you yet.'

My fury is unabated, and it fires me to speak again. 'Did you tame the tiger you turned into a rug? Is that what you have in mind for me?'

His hand snaps out and cracks me a stinging blow across my ear. I refuse to cry out or reach up to rub it, but Miss Wallace draws me closer to her, as if in protection.

His voice is cold and not directed at me, when he speaks again. 'Miss Wallace, I fear her life is too easy here. Comfort cannot win her round, it seems, so let us see what drudgery does.' He turns once more to me. 'You will change your present finery for a servant's smock. You will move into the basement scullery, where you will work every hour you are awake. And you will do so until your fires of rebellion have guttered out. Then we will see if you know how to speak to my guests and to me.' And with that he spins on his heel, and strides back down the corridor.

❦

Abigail hunched over her homework, neatly laid out on the bedroom desk. Her maths textbook lay open at a page of of exercises, and her notepad was almost filled with carefully arranged equations and diagrams and symbols in different-coloured inks, the result of months of diligent homework.

'Abigail!' her mother called from downstairs. 'Don't work too late!'

Abby didn't reply at first, but took her ruler and drew a thick black line under her work. She was careful to make sure it would not smudge before she closed the book. 'I've finished,' she said over her shoulder, but her mother was already at the door. She'd been so intent on completing her homework correctly she hadn't heard the footsteps on the stairs.

'How was it tonight?' Her mother was in a chatty mood.

Abigail packed her books into her schoolbag, ready for the next day. 'OK.'

Her mother smiled. 'How did you do with the last lot?'

'I got a B. I made a few mistakes.'

'But that's great, Abby. Last term, before Christmas, it used to be all Ds and Es and Fs – if you did it all.'

'If I work harder I'll catch the mistakes and I'll get an A.'

'Glad to hear it. But that's enough for tonight, hmm? It's after nine – Tablet Time.' She disappeared to the bathroom and returned with two capsules and a glass of water, which she handed to Abby. She watched closely – pretending not to – as Abby placed the capsules in her mouth and took a gulp of water in a well-practised routine.

Her mother rattled the bottle. 'We're nearly out. We'll have to go back to the doctor soon.'

Abby opened her mouth wide to show the capsules

had gone. 'I thought it was automatic. You know, a repeat prescription.'

'It is. But every three months the doctor wants to see you to check you've not gone green.'

Abby looked down at her hands. 'I haven't.'

Her mother sighed. 'It was a joke, Abby.'

'Oh. Is it three months already?'

'It is. Do you not remember? I took you along just after you – just after the school play.'

'Don't remind me.

'But that shows how much the tablets are helping you – as well as what can happen if you don't take them. And it's no coincidence that your marks have got so much better. We're due back at the doctor next week. What's the best day for you?'

Abby shrugged. 'It doesn't matter. They're all the same.'

'You know what I mean, Abby. You musn't miss any tests.'

'I don't have any. Not this week.'

The worst of the winter is over, but the frosts still strike and it is dark for hours after I am roused by the cook.

My mattress is squeezed into an alcove in the scullery, where I struggle to find warmth under my thin blankets. I am glad that my first task on rising is to rake out yesterday's fire, and build a new one for breakfast and all the hot water the waking household requires. I have done it so many times now I do not need to be fully awake, for which I too am glad. I am worked so hard, and for so long, that I go to bed exhausted and wake little refreshed.

My daily tasks differ little: heat the water, peel the potatoes, scrape and chop the carrots, boil the dirty linen, iron and fold the clean, wash the pots and pans and glasses of last night's dinner and make ready for tonight's, polish the silverware, and more, and more, in an endless round. And through it all I speak to no one and no one speaks to me.

I know it is February, but not the date or the day of the week, and this is all I know of time. If I had a life before this scullery I scarcely recall it, and I have no room within me for any hope of a life after it. When I think of my mother, or of Calum, it is with a pain that has grown fogged by fatigue. I am a drudge. I have always been, and will always be, a drudge. It is my fate.

Chapter 6

Miss Wallace places a steadying hand on my arm as she knocks on the door to Colonel Williams' library. 'Enter,' he booms, and when we do it is to the one room in the house I have not yet seen. Leather-bound books line the walls to well above my height. A huge globe sits in its mahogany frame on one side of the fire, while on the other a large desk is strewn with open books and journals. And at the table sits Williams.

He lays down a heavy gilt fountain pen amid a pile of stamps and envelopes and thick cream writing paper. He stretches backwards, warming himself in the fire's glow as we approach. He seems in good humour, but Miss Wallace still halts a careful distance away before she speaks.

'Pardon my intrusion, Colonel, but Elisabeth has a request I think she should present in person.'

'Oh?' Intrigued, he gets to his feet. I remind myself not to give in to fear or fury, but simply to deliver the words I have rehearsed as I went about my daily tasks. I want him to believe I soften towards him, and will bend to his will, so I wait for him to indicate that I should speak.

He waves his hand indulgently, and I begin. 'Some time ago, Colonel, you said I might write to my . . . to my mother.'

He raises an eyebrow. 'Indeed I did. I would not wish you and her to lose contact, though your life lies here these days.' He smiles down at me and lays his hand on my shoulder. I work to suppress a shudder, and conjure a smile in return, as he runs his fingers through my hair and continues, 'We have more in common than you might imagine.'

I want this unwelcome contact to end, so I reach in my pocket for the letter I prepared days ago but could not send for want of stamps and access to the post. I sense Miss Wallace stiffen beside me. She does not like surprises, and I did not tell her, when I asked to see the Colonel, that my letter was already written.

He takes it from me, and cannot hide his momentary frown when he sees it is sealed. He returns to his desk and picks up a silver letter opener in the shape of a slender ornamental dagger. He slips the tip into the folds of the envelope, inspecting my face for a reaction. 'You do not object?'

I offer a little bow of my head. 'I had meant it for my mother's eyes only,' I tell him, 'but there are no secrets within.'

He gives an approving nod and opens it, as I knew he would. I wait, stilling myself as best I can, and I watch his eyes as they scan my letter. The noises of the room grow loud to fill the silence while he reads: his leather boots creak as he shifts his weight, the mantelpiece clock ticks oh-so-slowly, a log shifts in the fireplace.

He interrupts his reading to look at me with a widening smile. 'I had wondered if you were simply weary of your daily drudgery and your scullery bed but I begin to believe you are coming round, Elisabeth.' And with that he turns the page and reads on, until his eyes sink inside another frown. 'But what is this?' he asks me, pointing to the last few lines.

'It is Gaelic, sir.'

'I know that. I recognise the language of rebels and outcasts readily enough. But what does it say?'

I am braced for the lie. 'It is drawn from a song. Words of comfort at a time of farewell. It is our customary way to say goodbye.'

'Indeed.' He turns away abruptly. 'Will you translate, Miss Wallace?'

My chest clenches suddenly and I cannot take a breath. For I gambled that she is a lowland Scot and would lack a knowledge of Gaelic. I gambled – and I have lost!

She takes the letter hesitantly. 'I have forgotten

much, Colonel, through lack of use. I do not know if I can.'

'Whatever you are able,' he tells her in a level tone.

There is another silence, longer and louder than the first, as she studies the lines. When she is done she raises her head and looks at me with a sadness I have not seen in her eyes before. She hesitates.

'Well?' he demands.

'Colonel –'

'What does it SAY?' His voice is louder now and his smile has gone. He fingers the dagger.

Miss Wallace cannot look at me as she relays my words. 'She says she is slowly dying here in this house, this city. She gives your address and pleads for rescue. She says she will never submit and be what you want her to be.'

His movements are so fast they are completed before I can react. He pulls me forwards and pins my palm against his desk with the blunt tip of the dagger. With his other hand he rips the letter from Miss Wallace's grasp, crumples it into a ball, and hurls it into the fire. The flare from my burning words illuminates the cold fury in his face as he glares at me.

The pressure on my hand increases, and I look down to see the point of the letter opener press ever deeper. My fingers flutter amid the stamps and pens and pretty parchment, like the wings of a pinioned butterfly.

Miss Wallace steps forwards. 'Colonel —' she pleads. To know I will not plead for myself only fires his fury further, and he strikes me full across the face with the back of his free hand. One of his rings draws blood, and I taste its salty stickiness through the stinging pain.

Miss Wallace cries out. 'Colonel! I fear you go too far!'

'SILENCE, WOMAN!' he commands. 'This ungrateful wretch condemns my efforts, my desire to see her lot in life improved, my household and me. She lies and deceives and seeks to return to the miserable hovel she calls home. I shall not give her that satisfaction. Go too far? I have clearly not gone nearly far enough in breaking her rebellious Highland spirit. And break it I will.'

At last he releases my captured hand, and points the dagger at me and Miss Wallace in turn to emphasise his words. 'Does she – do you – forget why my regiment was sent to her cursed island? We broke the Highland rebellion then, and I will break hers now. And henceforth, Miss Wallace, far from speaking up as her protector, you will double her labours and not bring her back before me until she knows her place.'

He raises his fist to strike me again and, despite his warning, Miss Wallace steps forwards and grabs his arm. I shriek, and throw myself forwards on his desk, my hand protecting my head. I make much noisy show of begging him not to hit me again.

No new blow falls, and when Miss Wallace pulls me upright I see Williams has retreated to stare fiercely through the window. He ignores us both. I straighten slowly, rubbing my injured hand against my injured face. I say nothing, and clutch at my dress with my free hand as I am bundled out of the room. Neither Williams nor Miss Wallace see the parchment I have stuffed into my dress, or the stamps I have picked up with my tongue, in my pretended pitiful writhings on his desks. For I am resolved that no one but my mother shall see the next letter I write.

Abigail's father looked over her bent head at the timetable stuck on the wall above her desk. 0645 Alarm clock. One five-minute snooze; 0650 Get up and go over list for the day; 0700 Shower.

He lowered his gaze and stepped forwards to peer over her shoulder. 0715 Get dressed; 0725 Let Muppet out into garden; 0730 Breakfast: cereal, toast and tea. Always finish old jam before opening new one.

Usually her desk was covered in an orderly array of schoolbooks, pens and pencils, rubbers and rulers. Now there was just an exercise book, open at the first double page. Abigail's pen was poised but the pages were empty.

0745 Clean teeth; 0755 Clean shoes; 0800 Check bags and schoolbook; 0810 Let Muppet back in.

'Are you stuck there, Abby?' he asked gently. These days it was unusual to see her struggle with homework. 0815 listen to weather forecast. Take coat if more than twenty per cent chance of rain. 0820 Leave for school; 0830 memorise dates for history on way through park.

She straightened up and turned, nodding gravely. She didn't speak.

'What is it? Maths? French?'

She shook her head. 'It's a project.'

'Oh. What kind of project?' 0845 Arrive at school. Unpack books and prepare for first lesson. 0900 Lessons start – see separate timetable in school desk.

'It's called an Imagination Project. It's for History or Geography. If we want we can use it for both.'

'And what are you supposed to do?'

'Whatever we want. They're going to give us some ideas on Wednesday, but they wanted to see what ideas we had first.'

'I see.' He looked at his watch. She'd been here for an hour. He didn't want to ask if she been staring at her book for all that time.

'I don't have any ideas,' she said flatly. 'They don't come any more. I miss them, Dad.'

She looked from his blank face to her blank page, and then out of the window. 'Ideas, I mean.' She didn't add that she also missed the other worlds she used to visit, and the people she could be in them. All that was left to her now was Morag – and she was trapped in a life of labour in London.

He laid a hand on her shoulder. 'I miss them too, Abby.' When she turned back to him, her eyes were moist. He looked away and scanned the walls. Her after-school timetable continued on a separate sheet, in a mirror image of the morning. Even her dog was timetabled. On the drawers nearby stood a framed photograph taken at the rail of a ship, on the way to Mull the summer before. She was smiling and her hair streamed in the wind. Where was that girl now?

She looked up. 'Is it Tablet Time?' she asked.

'It is, Abby.' He sighed. 'But I tell you what. I don't need to see you take them. Not tonight. I'll just leave you to it, eh?" He turned and made for the door. 'Don't stare at that empty book much longer, will you?'

It is at last light in the mornings when I rise, though it is still cold enough for fires; and now, having finished in the kitchen, Miss Wallace has sent me upstairs to rake out the parlour fireplace. She works me hard, but these last weeks, since our encounter with Williams, I have sensed a warming within her, much as I feel the coming of distant spring.

I am alone in the room, and take the chance to pause a moment and to gaze from the window.

The garden grass has not yet begun to grow, and patches of mud show through here and there. The skeletal trees thrust bony fingers skywards, as if pleading with the sun to warm them. They stir in the breeze, which pushes ragged clouds across the sky and tugs streaks of smoke from chimneys near and far. I sigh that my world has shrunk to this: that a glimpse of wintry garden is all I know of the world beyond these walls. I turn away and bend to my labours.

The fireplace is deep, and the brick still warm, as I kneel and reach in to break up the crumbled coals and rake out the ash. A cloud of fine dust rises around me, to catch in my nose and throat. I sneeze, and as I do a flash of white catches my eye, at the very back of the grate.

I stretch to pluck it out from the powdery grey ash. It is a fragment of paper, part of an envelope, and when I turn it over there is writing. I wipe off the ash and peer close to read it, and am stunned to see my own name, in a hand I do not know.

Morag McGregor, C/o Col. Williams, Playfair Hall, Richmond Ave–.

I stare at the fragment, as if it will yield answers to the questions tumbling round my mind. In the letter I smuggled out to my mother a month ago I warned her not to write back, for fear of Williams' reaction, but who else knows I am here? And what have they said?

There are footsteps in the hall. I hurriedly pocket the paper and return to my toil.

Abigail opened the bathroom cabinet and reached for the pill bottle in its familiar perch on the second shelf. She shook some capsules into her hand and stared at them for a time, then looked through the open door into her bedroom, where her exercise book lay empty on the desk. Her fist curled around the capsules.

She closed the bathroom door and locked it behind her, then switched her electric toothbrush to high speed, set the taps running, and sat down to think.

She uncurled her hand and looked down at the capsules again. *You've stolen all my ideas*, she thought. *I've had enough of you*.

She was sure her mother counted the capsules; so if she wasn't to take tonight's dose she would have to get rid of them. But how? The window? It opened on to the garden: Muppet would be sure to hoover them up. The bin? There wasn't much in it: her mother would surely see when she emptied it later. Pyjama pocket? But then what?

Abigail dropped that day's two capsules into the toilet bowl and flushed it, then set about her teeth with her buzzing toothbrush. When she looked back into the toilet she froze, for there floated the capsules, unflushed, intact and accusing.

She grimaced as she stooped to dip her thumb and forefinger into the toilet water to pick out the capsules. This wasn't going to be as easy as she thought. But she would find a way.

I am astride a magnificent black horse as he thunders down a steep hillside towards a crescent beach. There is no saddle, and despite my desperate grip with hands and tweed-trousered knees I slip about on his back so violently I am surely soon to fall. Yet still I urge him on, and look over my shoulder. My hair streams behind me in a red trail above the rich black of the horse's tail. His hammering hooves fling clods of mud and divots of turf into the air as we descend, close under trees, leaping over low field walls and scattering panicked sheep before us, all a-bleat with fear.

The slope eases and gives way to the low dunes above the beach, where a gathered throng waves farewell to an offshore ship, now lowering her sails and slipping away to the west. Heads turn when they hear our approach, and they pull back from our path.

'Stop him!' rises a cry behind me and I look back again. In furious pursuit gallops a company of red-coated soldiers. A musket cracks.

Abby's third yawn of the morning drew her mother's attention.

'Tired, Abby?' she enquired. 'Didn't you sleep well?'

'Strange dreams,' Abby replied, between mouthfuls of cornflakes.

'Oh? That's unusual for you these days. A nightmare, was it?'

'Not exactly. I was riding a big black horse downhill to a beach. We were being chased. I was dressed in old-fashioned clothes. Boy's clothes.'

'Woooah there!' said Naomi, as she spread jam on to her toast. 'Your dreams are much more exciting than your waking life.'

Abby's father put down his mug. 'The same is true for all of us, Naomi. Even you, my girl.'

'Sorry,' said Naomi. She didn't look it as she leant forward with a conspiratorial air. 'At least we know what all the groaning was about though.'

Abigail protested. 'I was not groaning.'

'How do you know? You were asleep.'

'But I wasn't groaning in my dream. There was nothing to groan about. There were soldiers chasing us, but I was riding the best horse on the island and I wasn't scared. Even when they shot at me.'

Naomi put down her toast and changed her tone. 'There was shooting?'

'Only once. A warning shot. They weren't shooting at me. Anyway, that's when the dream stopped.'

Naomi turned to Abigail, suddenly serious. Abby couldn't tell if she was putting it on. 'Ohmigod,' she said. 'I heard it too. That's freaky, Sis. I heard what happened in your dream.'

Dad smiled. 'Don't be ridiculous, Naomi. You heard what happened in our street. There was a car backfired, right outside. Just once – at 3:47 a.m. When it woke me up I looked at the clock.'

Abigail sighed. 'Why is there always a sensible explanation?'

Her mother finished her tea and rinsed her mug under the tap. 'That's just the way the world is, Abby.'

She hung the mug on its hook, then turned to her daughter. 'But I'm more concerned about why you're getting strange dreams again. You've not had them for months, not since you started the tablets.' Her eyes narrowed as she approached the table. She sat down at the empty chair, right next to Abigail. 'Did you take your tablets last night, Abby?'

There was a pause while Abby thought what to say. Her mother didn't wait to hear her before she fired another question. 'Did you check, Dave?'

'No,' he replied. 'And I'm not sure we should be checking every night.'

Her mother turned her attention back to Abby. 'Well?' she demanded.

Abby swallowed hard. She hated deceit. 'I had some trouble getting them down, but I got rid of them in the end,' she said, doing her best to return her mother's interrogatory gaze. It wasn't an outright lie, and she hoped there wouldn't be any further questions which would require one.

'Hmm,' said her mother sceptically. 'I don't suppose

I have to remind you what happened last time –'

Abigail winced and looked away.

Her mother persisted. 'I'm going to check you take your tablets every night from now till your exams, Abby.'

'But that's months away,' Abby protested weakly, looking to her father for rescue.

'Is that really necessary, Alison?'

Her mother didn't reply, but motioned with her eyes to the kitchen door, and then followed him through it. Abigail and Naomi fell silent, doing their best to listen while appearing not to. To begin with all they heard were odd words and phrases – *trust* . . . *carelessness* . . . *we have to check* – but after a while the volume rose.

'I still cringe when I think back to that school play. All the other mothers staring at me.'

'And I cringe too – but on *her* behalf, not mine.'

'Well, if you're not checking every night, I will. She has to earn my trust.'

And then the front door slammed loudly. When their father drove off, moments later, he was gunning the engine hard. Naomi and Abigail exchanged glances,

They'd heard their parents row before, but never like this.

❧

The post is delivered twice daily, soon after breakfast and again before lunch. I try to time my tasks so I am always nearby when the postman rings the bell. If I cannot be outside, washing the step or polishing the brass work, then I will be within, dusting the banisters or sweeping the floor. At the very least I will be watching through a window or from the landing. A smile of greeting shows he has begun to notice me, though I have not yet dared speak to him. Miss Wallace is always nearby too. She does not seem to be watching, though I am sure she sees my every move; and she does not show that she listens, though I fear she would be upon me like a hawk if ever I ventured to make enquiries of the postman. And yet, if there has been one letter sent here to me, there can surely be another. I am determined to be at hand when it arrives. This time only I shall read it.

Today, when the postman is due, Miss Wallace sends me to the coal cellar. When I emerge my first glance is for the kitchen window, where I hope to see him. I press up close, careful not to mist up the panes, however breathless with anticipation I feel. Yes! There he is, in his familiar uniform. But no! He is walking away, rummaging in his bag for the next house's mail.

I dash to the hall, to see Miss Wallace turning away from the closing door and making for the library with the Colonel's mail. Halfway there she stops and takes an envelope from the pile. She studies it, then looks around to ensure she is unobserved. She does not see me shrink back through the kitchen doorway; but I see her as she slips the letter into the folds of her dress.

I have to be sure, but I know she will show me nothing, so I turn and race out through the back door to the street. Here I stop and stare about for a glimpse of the postman's uniform – and there, above a wall, I glimpse the very peak of his cap as he moves on round the corner.

'Excuse me, sir!' I call, as I turn the corner after him and run on until I am at his side. 'Excuse me!'

He pauses, turns, and bends towards me with a smile. 'Orl right, young 'un?' he says, in a broad cockney accent. I have heard it enough now to understand him, though I like it none the better.

'My name's Morag. Morag McGregor. I live in –'

'So *you're* the mysterious Morag. I know where you live.'

'Was there – was there a letter for me today?'

'Too right, dear. Another one. Every week they've been coming, for ages now. And a long road they travel too. All the way from Scotland. Aintcha ever replied?'

And now the tears well in my eyes, from different reservoirs of feeling: warm joy that someone knows where I am and is trying to contact me, cold fury that I have been denied that contact; and a flickering hope that I might yet escape and find my way home.

'Oh, I see,' says the postman, gently. 'Can't write, eh?' He rubs away the tear that runs down my cheek, and gives me a gap-toothed smile. 'Well, I reckon you've got time to learn, 'cos whoever's sendin' them letters don't look like they'll ever give up.'

The first signs – odd beeps and clicks, whirrs and whistles – were easy to miss. She heard them in the corridor, in the playground, in the dinner queue. At first she thought it was some new ring-tone; but no one ever answered a phone. Then she wondered if it was the security cameras the school had installed. It wasn't until one particularly prolonged burst of noise in the dinner queue was followed by a ripple of cruel laughter that she realised the source was her fellow pupils, and it was directed at her.

The noises followed her throughout the school day, accompanied by staccato mechanical movements and blank-eyed stares, from those around her, as if she was classmate to a gang of robots.

One afternoon, returning to her desk after the last lesson, she found the whole class engaged in it. They trundled between the desks, twittering like *Star Wars* robots. Some blared 'Exterminate!' in Dalek voices and others clanked towards her as if she was facing the invasion of the Cybermen.

Abby opened her desk, surrounded by a phalanx of mocking robots, and struggled to appear calm while she sorted her books for homework. *At least they're bored with the zombie taunts*, she reassured herself. *But maybe they've been doing the robot stuff all along*, she thought, *and I've been too dulled by those pills to notice*.

She got up, trying not to look at any of them, and especially not Elaine. As she made for the door, still striving to ignore them, her cheeks reddened, heated by the fires that raged within; fires of embarrassment and humiliation, and a burning determination to prove them all wrong.

The day passes even more slowly than usual now that I have additional cause to will nightfall forwards, but I use the time, and the tasks, to prepare. I sweep the hall, I polish the stair rods, I dust the banister, I burnish the brass of doorknobs and knockers. And everywhere I go I am testing with my feet and the weight of my body. I listen for the creak of loose boards, I count the gaps between safely silent stairs, and I measure in footfalls, again and again, the distances I must travel, till I have them memorised.

Towards the end of the day, when the house is quiet before the dinner preparations begin, and only the slow ticking of the heavy clock breaks the silence, I undertake the entire route from the scullery to the landing with my eyes tight shut. Four . . . five . . . six . . . I count as I near my destination. I reach forwards with my left hand, and am greeted by the chill brass of a doorknob. I open my eyes with a small smile of satisfaction, for I will be coming this way in the dark tonight, and the door before me is Miss Wallace's.

Abigail wandered along the shelves of the shop. She had most of what she wanted – icing sugar, tweezers, various kinds of glue – but she couldn't find the last item. She didn't know if they sold these things any more, or if they did, whether they'd sell them to her. She chose the most helpful looking shop assistant to approach.

'Excuse me,' she enquired with a smile. 'My grandad's sent me for razor blades and I can't find them. Have you got any?'

'The old-fashioned kind?'

'Yes.'

'Not much call for them these days, love – but you'll find them over there, aisle ten, near the top.'

Abigail nodded and smiled her thanks, but didn't move away. 'And can you tell me . . . can you eat any of these glues?'

The lady frowned, but Abby continued. 'I'm making cake decorations for my grandad – he's eighty soon – and I need glue to hold them together, and I don't want to drop any of it on the cake. I don't want to poison him on his birthday.'

The lady laughed. 'No, no, of course you don't, love.' She reached into Abby's basket. 'Here. This is the one you want. I use it on all the cakes in my family. Though there's some of them I wouldn't mind poisoning sometimes!'

❧

I lie awake, listening, till the last of the Colonel's dinner guests have gone and the sounds of clearing up have ceased. When the church clocks strike midnight I rise and slip my feet into the thickest stockings I can find. I wrap a woollen shawl round my shoulders, to ward off the shivers as I listen at the kitchen door.

I hear the rustle of early-leaved trees and the hoot of an owl in the garden outside. From further away comes the lonely bark of a fox on the common. I focus my hearing on the closer, smaller sounds of a house at night: the tick of a cooling stove, the crackle of embers and the sliding of ashes in the fireplace, the dripping of a tap. Behind it all is the leisurely but remorseless tick of the grandfather clock in the hall, louder than ever now. The house feels enormous but it also feels empty, for there is no sound of human movement. I open the door.

Chilly silver moonlight pours through the hall windows on to the chequerboard floor tiles. I take a breath and move forwards, stepping only on the black tiles, till I am at the base of the stairs, where I pause again to look and listen.

I decide to take the stairs without stopping and rehearse once more in my head which ones I must miss out. Halfway up something brushes against my legs and I freeze. I bend, slowly, to feel the tabby cat I cannot see against the pattern of the stair carpet. I stroke it once, more to soothe my own hammering heart than to greet the creature, and when it starts to purr I move on, grateful that the Colonel has no dog. I must remember the cat on the way back down.

I am outside Miss Wallace's room. I have never been inside, though I have spent my waiting hours tonight trying to guess its layout from its position in the building.

Miss Wallace is particular enough not to have a creaking door, and it swings smoothly open to reveal a bed where I thought it would be, a dressing table below the window, and a wardrobe to one side. She's pulled the curtains across, but not completely, and enough light spills through the gap for me to navigate across the floor. Her grey-brown tresses are laid out across the pillow as she sleeps, shining silver where the moonlight catches them. I have never seen her hair unpinned before.

A dress hangs ready on a screen between her bed and the window. I cannot tell if it is the one she wore that day or another laid out for the next: they all look so severely similar to me.

My heart thuds so heavily inside my chest I am sure it must wake her, but I will myself forwards, slowly and carefully, till I can reach the dress. I feel for the pockets and slide my hand within, only to find emptiness. I turn to the dresser. It is covered in tiny ornaments and unopened bottles of scent, and there are many little drawers. I open the first, and pull out the papers within. Some of the bottles chink together despite my care. It is difficult to read in the dim light, and it takes time and care, but one by one I replace the papers, as not meant for me, till the drawer is full, and I move to the next.

Miss Wallace stirs, and murmurs something in her sleep. I stand motionless, willing myself into a statue for what seems an age after her breathing steadies and she lies still, before I resume my search. The clocks are striking one as I reach for the last drawer, but it resists my coaxing fingers and refuses to open: it is locked, and the treasure I seek must be within. I struggle to quell my frustration, trying hard to think where she might keep the key.

'Here,' says a voice in the darkness. Miss Wallace. I am too far from the door to make a run for it. 'You want the key? Then approach. I have it here.'

She sits up in bed and lights a candle. With her hair down, and the candle light's glow, she looks younger and softer than the forbidding facade she shows the daytime world. She bows her head and slips from around her neck a green silk ribbon on which hangs a tiny silver key.

I do not – I cannot – move, though thoughts

race nimble-footed through my mind. *What does she mean to do?* I ask myself. *Will she tell the Colonel? Is this a trap?*

She speaks again. 'I knew they could not be kept from you forever.' She reaches out towards me. 'Your letters.'

She hears my gasp. 'That is what you seek, is it not?'

I nod.

'Then come and take the key.' The candlelight shows an absence of malice in her face, which encourages me to take the ribbon.

'Open it, and bring me the letters. Both sets.'

I obey. Inside the drawer are two bundles, different in size and in age, but both tied with the same kind of ribbon as that which bears the key. I return to her bedside and hand them over.

She weighs them in her hands, and indicates the heavier bundle. The paper is old, and faded, and worn. 'I know the value of letters, child, and have treasured these for years, though I have not looked at them since you came to this house.' She unties the ribbon and the envelopes spill across the bedclothes, in different colours of paper and ink, but always the same hand.

She holds them up to the candlelight one by one. 'See the stamps? The seals? The postmarks? Canada. Bengal. The Gold Coast. Matabeleland. Alasdair wrote to me from every continent, every corner of the Empire he served so loyally.'

She gathers them up again, with care, and reties the ribbon. 'But it was the Empire that took him. Not in a battle, covered in glory, but in a fever hospital, covered in flies. Just as his time was done and the Empire had agreed to give him up to his homeland, and to me.'

She lays the bundle aside and leans towards me. 'Scotland was his home, and mine, but the day I learnt of his death was the day I left, never to return until sent to collect you from those ruffian thieves.'

She raises the other bundle – my bundle. 'And

what should follow you but these. I tried to keep them from you for the sake of your poor mother, and from the Colonel for fear of his anger; but I knew it was wrong, and I knew there would be a time like this. So, here. Take them, Elis–. No. Take them, *Morag*. Read them. Treasure them.'

She passes them into my trembling hands. I want to race away and read them immediately, but I sense she has more to say, and I look up at her again.

'And then act on them, Morag, in whatever way you must. For if I have learnt anything in my long life it is that letters, however heartfelt, however precious, are not enough.'

Abby checked again that the bathroom door was firmly locked, then turned the volume up on the radio and slowed down the taps that were filling the bath.

She sat on the edge of the bath with the soap rack

balanced on her knees. Usually it held soap, flannels and a pumice stone, but now it bore her tools, laid out like surgical instruments. On the right hand end was the pill bottle, which she opened carefully so as not to raise a rattle. With a pairs of tweezers she gripped one of the fat capsules, as a fisherman might a maggot. She lowered it to the surface of a small round mirror and held it in place. She then picked up a razor blade, which she had wrapped with a plaster for safety. She pressed the blade against the capsule, right on the join between the pink plastic and the green. She squeezed down on the capsule which she allowed to roll slightly back and forth in the tweezers' grip, until the blade bit in.

She maintained the pressure and increased the rolling, until there was a tiny puff of powder – *maggot blood*, she thought – to show that she'd cut all the way through the capsule's coating. Now she extended the cut all the way round, until she had sliced the capsule neatly in half.

She picked up one half and up-ended it over the sink, tapping gently until all the powder had dropped out, then repeated this with the other half-capsule. She picked up a square of paper, folded it and ran her fingernail along the crease until it was as crisp as she could make it. She unfolded it again, shook a small pile of icing sugar into it, then picked up the paper by the two edges, so that the sugar fell into a line along the fold.

Holding this in her right hand, she picked up a half-capsule with the tweezers in her left and carefully filled it with icing sugar from the paper. Next she reached for the little tube of glue, which she smeared on to a small saucer. She picked up the remaining half-capsule with a second pair of tweezers, rubbed its cut end into the glue, then squeezed the two halves of the capsule together while watching the second hand of her wristwatch.

When a minute had gone by she tapped the re-united capsule against the mirror, fully expecting it to break open and spill its now-innocuous contents on to the mirror. It didn't.

Abigail smiled and checked her watch again. Three minutes twenty-five seconds. She counted the capsules in the bottle. Fourteen. This was going to have to be a long bath.

Once safely back in my scullery bed-space, and sure I have not been followed, I light the stub of a kitchen candle and untie the bundle with shaking hands. There are few clues on the outside as to the sender. The writing is not my mother's. *Could it be Calum?* I wonder, as the letters spill over my blanket.

I silently bless Miss Wallace when I see that the seals are unbroken and the letters unread, but I wonder if she saw all the contents of the one the Colonel burnt.

I look for dates on the postmarks, torn between reading them in the order they were sent and going straight to the most recent. Another chime of the church clock makes up my mind, and I carefully break the seal on the latest letter. As I unfold the paper, my eyes race to the very end. It is Calum!

And now I return to the top to race through his words. I have to re-read them twice more before I can take it all in.

> *Dearest Morag,*
>
> *I know you would reply if you could, so I fear your silence means my letters do not reach you. Things have worsened here. It will soon be Whitsun, when your mother is to be evicted, along with so many others on Mull. There is talk of a ship to take them all to Canada. Uncle Murdo and I are secure, if only for the present.*
>
> *If you receive this in time, and can find your way to freedom, I urge you to return as soon as you are able. I will be waiting for you.*
>
> *Calum*

I look to the calendar on the kitchen wall. Whitsun. I have three days.

Abigail started at the knock on the bathroom door. She lowered the soap rack to the floor, slipped off her dressing gown, and stepped into the bath, where she made much show of splashing, before turning the radio down and responding with an innocent 'Yes?'

'Abby, you'll dissolve if you stay in that water much longer,' said her mother through the door. 'Dinner's ready. Hurry up and come downstairs.'

'Sorry, Mum. I must have fallen asleep.'

'I don't know how you can, with that terrible music blaring out.' Her mother's voice retreated towards the stairs. 'It's enough to wake the dead.'

Abby washed, faster than ever before in her life, then pulled the plug and stepped out, not bothering to towel down before donning her dressing gown. She replaced the lid on the pill bottle and put the bottle in the cabinet, then set about tidying away all evidence of her activity. She taped the remaining edge of the razor blade, and slipped it into her pocket together with the icing sugar, the paper, her tweezers, the glue and the saucers. She wiped her mother's mirror clean, and put it away, then replaced the soap rack, opened the door, and called down the stairs, 'I'm ready!'

❧

There is a knock at the scullery door, barely noticeable but definite. It comes again, and I slip out of bed carrying my candle in one hand and Calum's letter, with its terrible news, in the other. The door opens before I reach it, and in steps Miss Wallace.

'I cannot sleep,' she begins. 'I fear for what these letters tell you, Morag. And judging by your face, the news is not good.'

I shake my head.

'You must leave?'

I nod.

'Now? Tonight?'

I nod again, and hand her the letter so she understands.

When she has finished she holds me by the shoulders and looks directly into my face, but with none of her former hardness. 'Go to her, Morag, and quickly. Your mother's plight is one I know all too well. She should not cross that ocean alone.'

She hands me a canvas bag from a hook on the wall. 'Pack what food you can into this. I'll be back shortly.' She steps into the nearby laundry room.

I rummage for bread and cheese and fruit, which I stuff into the bag. She is back by the time I am ready, and hands me the clothes she has brought. 'You must have these.' She unfolds the garments, to reveal they are for a boy of about my size. 'Cook's son left them when he joined the Army. She's kept them ever since. They are old, but they will serve. It is hazardous enough for a boy to travel alone. For a girl it is impossible.'

She holds out a pair of scissors and a cap. 'And your hair should be cut or capped. You choose.'

I take the cap. She smiles briefly. 'Hair such

as yours is easily remembered, Morag.'

'And you must take this.' She drops coins into the cap. 'But you must leave now. In another hour the house will be stirring. I will cover your absence as long as I can, but believe me, when the Colonel finds you gone, he will come after you. Remember his nature: he is a hunter. Tigers in cages bore him, but a tiger to chase – it is what he lives for.'

I nod at her to show I understand, while I quickly dress in the unfamiliar items. 'But why has he chosen me to hunt? Why am I his tiger?'

She shakes her head. 'I cannot bring myself to tell you. Hasten to your mother that you may ask her.' I pocket the coins from the cap and place it on my head. She tucks my hair underneath it, carefully. 'Now, remember he is a powerful man. He has the ear of the police, and the army, and who knows who else on your route. Railway men. Ferry men. Inn-keepers. He will offer a reward for your return.'

And now, when I am ready, she bends down to offer me a kiss. 'Be careful.' She straightens and backs away to the door, where she pauses, one hand on the doorknob. 'And greet Scotland for me.'

Chapter 7

*A*bby threw the ball for the twentieth time, and again Muppet crashed through the under-growth chasing it. He'd lost fitness during the sluggish months of winter, so he was slower and more easily tired, but his delight in Abby's renewed playfulness was obvious.

'Enough, Muppet.' Abigail rubbed her shoulder where it hurt from all the throwing, and pocketed the slobbery ball. 'That's enough for now.'

She snapped his lead on to the ring on his collar, and strode off towards the park gate. As she did she sensed an opening, a brightening inside her. Familiar and much-missed sensations – sounds, sights, smells, tastes – flooded in from another world as a window swung open in her head. She smiled in recognition and welcome. *It's coming back*, she thought. And this time I'm not going to lose it.

⁊

The first streaks of dawn smudge the eastern sky,
but the streets are still dark, except for the pools of
sickly gaslight glow. I keep to the half-light as much
as I can, wishing neither conspicuous illumination
nor the threat of tar-dark alleyways where thieves
and worse lurk amid the sprawling drunks.

I have been walking an hour or more, and am
getting used to the unfamiliar feel of trousers –
both freer and more encumbering than skirts at
one and the same time. My ill-fitting shoes
already pinch my feet. I carry a cache of letters
next to my heart, and the bag slung over my
shoulder is stuffed with my own clothes and the
food I stole from the Colonel's kitchen.

There are few people about, and most of
them are the early tradesfolk: milkmen and
fishmongers, barrow boys and flower girls.

Occasional horses clip past on errands of urgency, and once there was a coach, all lacquered black panels and shuttered windows. Already there are more souls on the street than when I first set out, but I do not know what carries more risk for me: the crowds of daytime or the city by night.

I am bound for a railway station, but I do not know which one I should seek, nor where it is, nor how to get there. I reason that because Glasgow is north and west of London, the station must be north and west of the city's centre, and Colonel Williams being the kind of man he is, he would not live anywhere other than the very middle. So, navigating by the Pole Star, I go roughly north-west from his house, or as much as the geography of the streets will allow me.

I feel again the cold roundness of Miss Wallace's coins in my pocket. I have no idea how far they will take me, nor what I will do when they are gone, but I know I have no choice other than to keep going. I shiver in the pre-dawn chill, pull my cap down harder, tighten my scarf, and stride on.

❧

'Tick tock,' said Naomi, as she slouched at the open door of the computer den.

'Five minutes?' Abigail pleaded. 'Just to finish this off?'

Naomi heaved a melodramatic sigh and looked at her watch with a theatrical gesture. 'At one second after five minutes I'm pulling the plug out, OK?' Abigail nodded, without taking her eyes off the screen, as Naomi finally let her curiosity show. 'What are you suddenly using it for anyway?'

'Nothing much. School stuff.'

Naomi tutted. Now Abigail looked at her. 'Well, at least I'm not e-mailing friends I've seen all day at school –'

'That's because you've got no friends –'

'– or going into boy-band chatrooms, or down-

212

loading rubbish music, or trying to sell my sister on e-bay, if that's what you mean.'

'You're just upset because no one bid for you.' Naomi flounced off, calling over her shoulder, 'That's four minutes twenty-one seconds left.'

The enormous station teems with more people than I knew existed, streaming in every direction, like worker ants driven from the comfort of their nests for a day of toil.

They all move with their eyes locked ahead, determined not to acknowledge each other's existence. It is as if greeting one fellow human would require a response to them all, in their heaving thousands, at the risk of being over-whelmed. None of them notices me, but I fear to approach any of them for directions lest I give myself away. The voice of a Scottish girl, in the dress of an English boy, would surely catch the attention of the most blinkered worker ant among them, and I do not want to find out whether the police are after me yet.

So I wander the vast space, trying to make sense of the thickets of signs directing me everywhere but home. Eventually I find a long wall bearing posters in glass cases: Destinations and Timetables, says a sign above them. I pass back and forth along the wall, scanning the dense type until the word Glasgow leaps out. I stop to stare at the poster, a grid of place names I do not know and numbers I cannot understand.

I step back to watch others consult neighbouring posters. I study the way they run their fingers across the rows and down the columns, mumbling to themselves and looking at their watches, then scribbling notes on fragments of paper. When I think I understand the method I step forwards again.

I trace my finger across from 'London St Pancras' to what must be a departure time:

08:40. I have no watch, but the huge station clock tells me it is now nearly eight. I run my finger down the column of arrival times till it is opposite my destination: Glasgow. I frown, for the number is 18:26, and I have not heard of eighteen o'clock. And then I tell myself what matters is that I get there, not when, and I set off in search of the ticket office.

In exactly four minutes twenty-two seconds Naomi was back. 'Tick tock tick tock tick TOCK!' she insisted, as she burst in and reached for the switch on the wall.

Abigail grabbed her wrist. 'NO!' she yelled. 'I'll lose it all!'

'Then save it, exit, and let me have my turn.'

'You've had sole use of this computer since Dad bought it. You can spare me a few minutes now.'

'I had sole use because you weren't interested. Now you want to take it over.'

'Enough!' Their father's voice behind them was stern. 'I bought the computer for all of us. If you two are going to fight over it like this, then neither of you can use it.'

There was a pause. Abby let go of Naomi's wrist and Naomi pulled back from the plug. 'Sorry, Dad,' they said together.

He looked at the two of them and shook his head. 'I tell you what. You get an hour each, on school nights.' Naomi sighed. 'And two hours on weekends. And that's a maximum, OK? I'll put up a booking sheet. You can take it in turns to go first, and I want a five-minute gap between you, when there's no one on it. Any more fights, I'll change the passwords so you can't use it at all.'

'Sounds OK to me,' said Abby. She looked up at her sister. 'I tell *you* what, Naomi. I'll look at the TV guide and book my hours when I know you'll be watching your rubbish telly.'

Naomi glared but did not speak. Their father smiled to himself, glad to see Abigail show some of her old spirit.

'And what are you working on, Abby?' he asked, once Naomi had left.

'Oh, nothing much. Just my Imagination Project. I've had an idea for it.'

'And?'

'Best not to say. Not yet. I don't know if it will work.'

The queue for the little ticket windows in the wooden wall moves slowly and, like most of those ahead and behind, my eyes are on the clock. *I must not miss this train*, we all chant, silently and separately. Of the three clerks working there I choose the middle one as the least forbidding.

I do not get him. 'Next!' comes the call from the window on the right. I stride up as casually as I can, studying the clerk's face. He reminds me of a weasel, with narrow chin, pointed nose and sharp little teeth, but thick glasses hide his eyes.

'Yes?' he snaps.

A Scottish voice asking for a ticket to Glasgow should not cause a problem if I make it gruff enough. 'Glasgow, please,' I growl.

'Singleoweturn?'

'What?'

'Single – or – return?' He spaces out the words and this time rolls the 'r's, but I still do not understand.

'What?'

He sighs and looks across to his fellow clerks, as if to say, *Got a right one here*. Then, very slowly, and very loudly: 'Do you want to come back?'

'No! No! Never!' I bluster when I finally understand. I hear restless impatience in the queue behind me, and realise I am being watched by an entire room full of people. I look out to the platforms, where a policeman stands, scanning the crowd.

The clerk sits back, enjoying his little piece of theatre. 'I know 'ow you feel, mate. I wouldn't come back neither. Now, what class?'

'What?'

'First, second or third? What class d'ya want?'

'Whatever gets there fastest.'

He laughs out loud at this, and I see the other clerks grinning. 'Aintcha been on a train before? They all get there the same time, mate, only some's more comfortable than others. It's funny though, the more comfortable you are, the faster the train seems to go. 'Ow much money ya got?'

I open my palm to show Miss Wallace's coins. His lips quiver as he makes a quick calculation. 'That'll buy ya a third-class single. Just. But it don't leave much to live on.'

I put the money in the little bowl under the grate through which we have been speaking. He takes it, and returns some farthings in change and the precious piece of paper that will transport me north. 'There ya go, son. 'eadin' 'ome, are ya?'

As I nod, fearing to speak any more lest there is another policeman behind me, a wisp of hair falls from beneath my cap and lies across my shoulder.

I quickly tuck it back up. The clerk has not seen it, but I cannot be so sure of the passengers behind me. I turn sharply from the window, tuck the ticket alongside my treasured letters, and drop the farthings into my trouser pocket, relieved that boys' clothes have so many more places to put things.

''Old on!' shouts the clerk as I hasten away. I fear he suspects me and think about running, but I choose instead to turn and face him.

'Platform fourteen, mate. You'll catch it if you're quick.'

I smile my thanks and run out, glad of the excuse to be in a hurry.

Abigail studied the shelves of the old shop. It was so small she could see everything without taking a step. She'd walked past with Muppet hundreds of times, but had never been inside until today. She'd never had a reason to.

She took a deep breath, drawing in the dry smells, the silence, and the beauty of the marbled paper on display.

'Can I help you?' said a white-haired lady.

'I hope so,' said Abigail. 'I'm looking for some special writing paper. It doesn't have to be fancy but it must look really old.'

'Hmm. Let's see, shall we?' She rummaged through sheaves and sheaves of paper, working steadily up the shelves. 'Aha!' she said to Abby's upturned face when she reached the very top.

Blowing off a decade's worth of dust, she laid a bundle on the counter – a half-sheaf of rough-textured yellowing paper, curling at the edges and flecked through with bits of grey.

'That looks good,' said Abby, 'but the edges are too sharp. Can you roughen it up a bit?'

The lady smiled. 'I'll leave that to you, dear. It was me who cut it so carefully years and years ago. How much would you like?'

'About ten pages.' Abby looked around at the gorgeous fountain pens in an illuminated glass box.

'What did they write with?'

'Who?'

'Ordinary people, a hundred and fifty years ago. Poor people.'

'They made their own pens.' She reached across to a large green feather, marked with a brilliant eye and sitting in a dried-up inkwell. 'Like this one.'

'Wow! Can you show me how?'

'You need a good feather from a big bird. This one's peacock, but a goose or a swan would do. And you need a very sharp knife. You cut the end like this . . . and then you slit it . . . like this.'

Abby peered closely, storing all the details in her magpie memory. The lady dipped the feather into the inkpot. 'Then you fill your inkwell, dip in your quill, and away you go. It's very messy.'

'Can I have a pot of old-style ink, please?'

The lady handed over a tiny glass bottle with rich dark-brown contents. 'Try this. It's called sepia.'

Abby fumbled in her pocket for her money. 'How much does it cost?'

The lady smiled her broadest smile yet. 'It doesn't cost money, dear. Just a promise that you'll bring your handiwork into my shop to show me when it's done.'

Abby grinned back and made for the door. 'Of course.'

'One more thing. When you collect the feathers, make sure there's not a bird still attached. Swans can be dangerous, you know.'

The train is packed, and I am so late in boarding it I cannot find a seat. I am forced to stand in an overheated carriage, surrounded by a crowd of tall men and unable to see anything other than the lapels and backs of their overcoats. Having not slept at all, and weary from walking and worry, I soon feel sweaty and sick and faint, and struggle against the rebellious buckling of my legs.

One of the men nearby notices this, and hauls me to my feet before I slip to the floor. 'All right, lad?' he asks.

I look up and nod to tell him I am fine, but my face must show I am not, to judge by the concern reflected in his. 'It's a long trip for standing in a crowd like this,' he says. 'There'll be seats after Birmingham, but that's a good few hours yet.'

He raises his hands above his head, and sets about rearranging the cases in the luggage rack. Then he stoops, and puts his hands together, with fingers interlaced, to create a kind of stirrup, which he lowers before my foot. 'Step aboard,' he urges, and I obey.

He raises me high, without apparent effort, till my head touches the roof of the carriage and I can scramble into the luggage-rack space he has created. I wriggle about to accommodate my shape to the jumble of cases, and soon have a kind of elevated bed. It may be hard, with corners that stick into me, and in a very public place, but it affords a view over the heads of the passengers and out through the windows, as well as the welcome chance of a rest.

'Thank you, sir,' I tell my protector, as I put my bag beneath my head for a pillow. He seemed a big man when I stood by his feet, but now, from high above the crowded carriage, I see his true stature. He stands head and shoulders above everyone else, and the seams of his enormous overcoat strain over his bulging muscles.

'What's your name, son?' he asks.

'Mor–' And I panic. I haven't given this a moment's thought. And now my mind is blank for boy's names. 'Mor– Mor– M–M–Mortimer,' I tell him at last. 'Johnny Mortimer.'

'A good sturdy name, that. I'm Bill. Bill Bailey. I'm a boxer. They call me the Brighton Bull. Pleased to meet you.' He holds up a monstrous and much-scarred hand. I stretch out mine, fearful lest it is too obviously that of a girl. He squeezes it so hard I am soon more fearful it will not be returned intact.

'Where are you bound?' he asks, and I realise, with a sinking feeling, that he means to engage me in chatter, which I cannot now avoid, being stationed not far from his head. I am not alert enough to lie convincingly for hours, so I feign a yawn when I say: 'Home.'

But the stifling heat of the carriage, and the movement of the train, and my lack of food and rest, bring on true sleepiness so quickly I do not have to feign it for long.

'There!' I point. The general and his jostling banks of massed horsemen now see what no man should ever set eyes upon: our secret mountain lake, known only to the women of my tribe, where inexhaustible schools of fish rise to our nets, where roofing reeds grow stout and strong, where the fabled goose lays its golden eggs. The day is windless and clear, and the lake as perfect as I have ever seen it: slate-smooth, and the deep blue of sapphires, of lapis lazuli.

At its very centre rises the island where the geese

nest every year. They always lay a clutch of seven eggs, the seventh being solid gold. When the new goslings hatch the golden egg fractures into a thousand nuggets, and when they first fly the nuggets transform overnight into scraps of feather, shards of shell. We have always known that if even one of the nuggets is taken the geese will depart, never to return, leaving the lake rancid, and sterile of fish, and fringed by blighted reeds.

Now, to my burning shame, I am captured by this general and his greedy men and forced to lead them to this treasure. When they tried to take my sword I resisted. 'Only death will part me from this sword,' I told them, 'And then you will never see the Lake of Fables.'

Their greed made them relent – which they will regret. For I must redeem the shame of this, my betrayal, and use my weapon, Gladriel, to visit her curse upon as many of them as I can take, beginning with the general. And I must hope and pray that the warrior women of my tribe even now watch and await my signal.

I adjust my leather armour and lower my hand to

Gladriel's heavy hilt, so familiar to my palm. I curl my fingers around it and take the weight, ready to draw the shining blade from her scabbard. And I wait until the general smiles indulgently, and allows his impatient men to dismount and splash into the water. It will be easier to take them there.

I close my eyes and draw my warriors close in my thoughts, willing my hope into truth, my faith into fact. I must believe. For when I free this sword and raise it overhead, if it does not summon an army of fearsome fighters, if it does not bring down a hail of poisoned arrows, if it does not raise our fearsome battle cry of death to all who intrude here, then it is not just I who am doomed but my family, my tribe, and the entirety of our history in this place.

I grip the sword tight and unsheath it, to hold it with both hands, high overhead, where its burnished blade shines and flashes in the evening sun. I –

'Stop it!' Abigail slapped her brow with the flat of her hand to admonish herself for drifting off again. She crouched beside a small willow tree, near the edge of the park's scruffy pond. Litter clogged the long grass at her feet, and closer to the water goose droppings mingled with mud. Some metres offshore three dozy geese paddled aimlessly about between the floating cans.

On the shore nearby, screened by a low fence, was the place where they nested, and though it was too early for eggs they were clearly getting protective, especially the largest one, a one-eyed male prone to angry hissing.

Abby had already circled the pond twice, scouring the shore for feathers and not finding any. There were feathers a-plenty strewn about the nesting site, but she didn't dare cross the fence with the geese so close. Not with those huge orange beaks ready to snap at her ankles. She just had to wait. She cursed herself for not bringing bread to tempt them away, or Muppet to drive them off.

A roar rises all around the lake at the sight of Gladriel unsheathed, and it is loud and fierce enough to frighten even me. The sky darkens with hissing arrows and my warriors race forwards, ululating fearsomely.

The men in the water turn in panic as the first arrows hit home, and then flounder shorewards. I lower Gladriel till she is held straight out from my shoulder, and I run directly at the general before he can overcome his shock. I plant my sword in the very centre of the huge red cross he wears on his tabard and his eyes widen further yet, with more than just surprise now. 'Thus is your greed repaid!' I yell at him before the light goes out of his eyes, and he slumps, dead, at my feet.

Abigail clapped her hand to her forehead again, harder this time. 'STOP it!' she commanded. 'Just concentrate, will you? There's a job to be done.'

As she settled back into waiting, she smiled to herself. *Maybe I should take a real tablet from time to time*, she mused. She was glad other world-windows were opening to her again, but that last one was a bit extreme. No! she went on. *I just have to be more in control, that's all.*

There was a sudden honking and splashing as the geese paddled off across the pond. On the far side a mother and toddler were tossing yesterday's crusts into the stagnant water, attracting a flurry of starlings and seagulls. The two smaller geese sped up, hoping to see them off before all the bread was gone. Abigail didn't notice the big male goose hanging back to check on her as she scampered forwards, jumped over the fence and quickly gathered up four or five of the biggest feathers, but she did hear his whirring wings as he raced ashore. She turned and ran. The goose pursued her, his neck extended, honking furiously and snapping his beak, till Abigail cleared the fence with a hurdler's ease and was safe.

‘Oi!’ I am roused roughly from dreamless sleep by a sharp dig in the ribs. ‘Wot d’yer fink yer doin’ up there, sonny?’ I look blearily around the carriage. Bill has gone, as have most of the passengers. The train clanks slowly through the fringes of some city or other. ‘Get dahn right now.’

I clamber down, nearly forgetting my bag. ‘Ticket, sonny. Ticket.’ The inspector thrusts his hand at me, obviously expecting me not to have one. I reach into my pocket and draw it out. I hand it over and study the two strange bits of card that came out of my pocket with it. The inspector struggles to hide his disappointment, and bounces back on the attack. ‘Luggage racks is for luggage. Not people. Not boys looking for a lazy bed. Wot’s wrong wiv ahr seats, eh? There’s loads of ’em empty.’

‘They were full in London.’

‘Don’t give me none of yer lip, lad, or I’ll sling

yer orf at the next stop. D'yer get up there yersel' or was yer 'elped?'

Now that I have identified the bits of card I feel emboldened enough to look him in the eye. 'Bill Bailey put me there.'

'Gerrahtofit! Bill Bailey? The Brighton Bull?'

I hand over the cards — tickets to a heavy-weight championship fight three days from now. 'Here. I can't go.'

His eyes swell, and he is suddenly speechless. He takes my arm and sets off along the aisle. I stumble after, worried that he really does mean to throw me off the train. But he leads me through to the next carriage, to second class, which is divided into compartments rather than open-bench seating. The first compartment is empty, and he draws me in.

'Why didn't yer say? Any friend of Bill's is a friend of mine. This whole compartment's yours, all the way to Scotland.' He makes to leave, but cannot resist a parting command. 'Just keep yer feet orf the seats, will yer?'

Abby's mum stood at the door of the computer den and shook the pill bottle. 'Time's up, Abby,' she said.

Abby hummed loudly to cover up the noises coming from the computer. 'OK, Mum. I'm done.'

Her mother couldn't quite make it out, but she thought she heard the puff and whistle of a steam train. And earlier in the evening, she was sure there'd been fiddle music, and a haunting song in a strange language. 'What are you up to anyway?' she asked.

'It's just – it's exercises, to get us using the computer. Is it Tablet Time?' Abigail asked innocently, as the screen went blank.

'Yes. And we're nearly out. That's why I'm taking you back to the doctor tomorrow.'

Abby groaned.

'You know he needs to see you every few months.'

'I've been trying to forget.'

'And this time there'll be a blood test.'

Abby's heart froze. 'Blood test?'

'Yes, dear. It's nothing special.'

'I know, but . . . what's it for?'

'I know to look at you you're healthy enough and these tablets are working a treat; but the doctor wants to be sure they aren't doing any hidden harm and that there's the right amount in your system.' She handed Abby one of the capsules and a glass of water. 'Now, get that down you, brush your teeth, and off to bed before my film starts.'

Abby stared at the capsule with its secret contents. *Everything's been going so well*, she thought, *and now they're going to discover what I've done, how I've fooled them all. And I've not finished yet.*

I watch the scenery slide by my window, glad to have escaped the endless grime of the cities. Birmingham, Manchester, Crewe and the rest were all grubbily identical, and between them the English countryside, though pretty enough by contrast, appears tame to me. The fields are small and neat, the hedgerows and copses tidily trimmed, and the lambs skip in their greening meadows as if they need not fear frosts or gales or the attentions of eagles, as they must on Mull.

I seem to have been travelling forever – long enough to finish all my food and to read and re-read Calum's letters. I urge the train on faster. *Take me to Scotland!* I tell it. *Speed me there.*

And soon it seems my request has been answered, for the landscape is changed and familiarly wild. Round-shouldered mountains, treeless and steep, loom high over long narrow lochs, spilling scree from their snow-dotted slopes. I sit up, suddenly more interested, as the ticket inspector passes. He brings only disappointment.

'Lovely, innit?' he chirps.

'It is. We must be in Scotland.'

'Don't be daft, lad. It's the Lake District. In Engerland. Aintcha got enough scenery of yer own? Yer wanter steal ahrs an' all?' He hands me a bread roll from the restaurant car. 'We're an hour from the border and Glasgow's an hour beyond that.'

I wonder what a border looks like, not having been awake when we crossed it on the way down. I picture a chain of stone cairns, a ditch dug in the hillside, marks painted on fences or cut into trees. But when it comes it is no more than a sign beside the track that says simply 'Scotland'. I turn as we speed past, to see 'England' written on the other side.

I'm on my way, I tell myself, and will my thoughts on to my mother and to Calum. *I've reached Scotland without capture.* I'll be with you soon. I only hope it is soon enough.

After the morning's last lesson Abigail raced out of the classroom, into the chaos of the playground, and through the gates. She only slowed to a walk when she was halfway down the high street. She waved at the lady in the window of the paper shop, then crossed the road to the garish lighting and ugly orange colours of the Internet Cafe.

She went straight to the counter, 'Do you burn CDs?' she asked.

Glasgow is colder than London, though not so dark at this time – eighteen o'clock – of the evening. Recent rain slicks the cobbled streets outside the station when I emerge. It is with relief that I look up to skies that are now clear. It will be a cold night, wherever I am to spend it, but at least it should not be wet.

I look around the thronged streets and savour the accents around me – different from the speech I know on Mull but recognisably Scottish. I taste the sweet smell of chestnuts roasting at a nearby stall, and enjoy it briefly before I feel it make my hunger pangs worse. I have no idea where to go now. Mull is still a hundred miles away, and I have no money for a fare. I have directed my thoughts so firmly towards Glasgow I have not got beyond the point were I now stand.

And then, turning left, I see the river, swirling oily and dark under the bridges in the twilight. *Rivers run to the sea*, I reason. *So I may as well follow it.* I pick my way to the riverside path, and turn to follow the glutinous water downstream, as it slides along between stone quaysides and under road and rail and footbridges.

The city here turns its back upon its river, even though it is the water that has brought the riches so evident in the fine buildings above me. I do not mind much, for it means I can make my way unimpeded by people, though fences and parapets and sudden sheer drops do their best to block my way.

All the while I look around, seeking some

kind of shelter for the night, and ever hopeful for food. I am hungry and tired, and already I grow cold, but none of these matches my apprehension about how I will pass the rest of my journey or what I will find when it ends, and this drives me on. *They might as well try to fence off water*, I tell myself, in a bid to raise my spirits, as I scramble over yet another barrier. *I am as unstoppable as this river.*

❧

Abigail bared her arm in silence. Her mother addressed the doctor. 'She's more bothered by needles now, but apart from that she's fine.'

Dr Smith looked at Abby as he applied a rubber band around her upper arm. 'No side effects?' he asked.

Abby shook her head. She couldn't take her eyes off the long steel needle he had unsheathed.

'None,' said her mother.

'Best not to watch,' the doctor said.

Abby felt a pressure, and then a sharp jag, and then a strange kind of buzz. She looked down to watch as the vacuum in the tube sucked her blood out in a thin red stream to splash against its plastic sides.

'Keep very still now,' he said, as he swapped the red-labelled tube, now full of blood, for an empty green one.

'There.' He untied the rubber band, withdrew the needle, and applied a piece of cotton wool in a smooth, well-choreographed movement. He obviously did this a lot.

She looked up at him as he pressed his thumb into the crook of her elbow. 'So these tests tell you if there's medicine in my blood?'

'They do more than that. They tell us exactly how much. So we know if we've got the dose right.'

Abby frowned. 'But surely . . .'

'Yes?'

'Surely, if it's doing what it's meant to, and it's not making me ill, you don't need a blood test. You just *know* the dose is right.'

The doctor smiled. 'A good point. You're pretty sharp, aren't you?' he added.

Her mother broke in. 'I can tell, Abby, from watching you, and from talking to the teachers, that Dr Smith has got the dose just right. The blood test's a precaution, that's all. Why are you making such a song and dance about it?'

'My teachers?'

'Yes, dear. Only yesterday they told us you're doing really well. They expect a lot from you in the exams next month. It's only your project they're concerned about. They haven't seen any of it yet.'

The doctor sealed the blood tubes in clear plastic bags, then reached across to Abby's arm. He took the cotton wool, with its vivid splash of red against the white, and pressed a little round plaster over the spot. He smiled again. 'Well done, Abby.' She didn't know if he meant the exams or the way she put up with his own tests.

Abby rolled her sleeve down, and turned back to her mother, with a harder edge in her voice. 'What then?' she asked.

'What d'you mean, dear?'

'Let's say I do OK at these exams. What then?'

The doctor broke in. 'More exams, I'm afraid. If you're good at them they never stop. I'm three times your age and I took my last exam a year ago.'

'So the reward for passing exams is to take more of them?' Abby scoffed. 'Is it worth it?'

The doctor looked flustered. 'Of course it is,' he said, unconvincingly.

'Abby!' her mother scolded. She hurried to change the subject. 'When do these results come through?'

The doctor seemed relieved to be back on safe ground. 'The basic tests – a day or two. The blood level takes longer. It should be back at the end of next week. I'll call you.'

Abby's heart soared. She'd assumed she'd be found out immediately, and she'd just been given a stay of execution for another week.

I huddle in the woodpile, my hands jammed into armpits to stop my fingers freezing off. Church clocks tell me it is after midnight but not yet one, so I have hours yet till daylight brings any hope of warmth, or food, or a way out of this city.

In the gaps between the rough-hewn planks that make my shelter, I gaze with envy on the watchman. He has a tiny wooden hut, like a sentry box, and before it burns a brazier, whose flickering flames illuminate his ungrateful face as the sparks rise above him. Every half-hour or so he stirs himself to wander round this cluttered dockyard, checking the tethered vessels and the quayside piles of goods. It is all I can do not to rush over, the moment he walks away, and spread my hands before his brazier's healing warmth.

But I know I cannot risk capture, for my mother's sake as much as my own, and I must stay here, enduring the splinters and the incongruously clean smell of pine, however cold I may get. I lay my head against the chilly wood and look at the patchy planking overhead. *If I have any good fortune left*, I tell myself, as I close my eyes, *it is that there has been no rain.* At that moment a rat runs over my toes.

Dawn comes with painful slowness, like a developing bruise. When the watchman finally departs, embers still glow red and orange in his brazier. Once I am sure he is not coming back I steal stiffly over to soak up the blessed heat. I raise one foot at a time, holding them close to the brazier till the leather scorches, and I hold out my hands as long as I can before withdrawing them to rub against each other and my numb, lifeless face.

As the daylight rises workmen and sailors begin to trickle into the yard, so when my hands and feet are at least half-thawed I set off to patrol the quayside and find myself a vessel.

There are coal boats and herring boats and timber boats, each with their characteristic smells. There is also the dung boat, moored alone and unloved some way off, but still making its presence felt.

Some of the craft are powered by sail, some by steam, and some by an uneasy mixture of the two. I know which I want, and I search among the rows of puffers – tough, broad-beamed vessels with a stout funnel near the stern. I have seen them visit Tobermory and Salen and Fishnish, and plying the Sound to the outer islands. There must be one among this fleet to carry me home.

I walk up and down the quayside, calling down to the increasingly busy decks of the boats below. 'Any hands needed?' I enquire again and again, and am always rebuffed. There are sullen shakes of the head, and indifferent shoulder shrugs, and there is laughter at my stature and the eagerness that masks my desperation.

And then I realise my mistake, for all the craft I have tried are Glasgow registered, as their painted sterns attest. And if they are about to leave their home port, they will all be fully crewed.

Now I search among them for any vessels from Mull or Coll or Tiree, but I find none until, as hunger digs hard in my belly, I try the next basin along and there she is: the *Sally*, of Tobermory.

I am about to hail her skipper, as he works alone on deck, when another idea strikes and I turn away. I pace up and down, dredging my memory for the words, so long unused, until I have them in some kind of order.

I stand at the top of the ladder that drops down to the deck. 'Failte,' I say. He looks up, as I knew he would, for no Glasgow urchins have the Gaelic tongue.

And I call to him, in the best Gaelic I can muster, 'Is there a deckhand you're needing, Captain?'

He looks up but says nothing. I continue. 'I am your man. I can haul ropes, and shift stores, and cook eggs as well as any man in Glasgow.'

Still he does nothing but stare, sizing me up, while I jabber on. I will even catch fish for your supper if you will but offer me bread and a berth.'

He shades his eyes from the low morning sun, against which I have carefully placed myself to minimise scrutiny. He pauses and I wait, feeling myself grow faint. I have no other ploy, no alternative plan. He is my last hope. He must take me on; he simply must.

And he waves me down.

Chapter 8

ally rides the ebbing tide down the Clyde to the open sea, the smoke from her funnel rising to the high, clear sky. The river is thick with activity. At first the shores are docks and warehouses and chimneys, but these soon give way to fields studded with mournful cows, and then to wide mudflats, with the dark bones of dead boats poking up through the ooze. The channel here is marked by high stone cairns, from which cormorants and shags watch the passing traffic.

There is little for us to do other than steer, which Skipper McAndrew reserves to himself, and keep watch, which falls to me. All I've done since we cast off at Glasgow has been to watch the water, while mugs of hot sweet tea and the greasy richness of a bacon roll work their miracles.

Ahead and to starboard rises the huge guardian crag of Dumbarton Rock, soaring directly from the river's edge to tower over us and the buildings clustered at its foot. And from these buildings there drift towards us the sounds of hammering and sawing, and the smells of paint and tar and fresh-cut wood. For here too are the skeletons of ship exposed, but these are the spines, the ribs, the breastbones of vessels under construction. One of them, nearly finished, rises like a cathedral, with masts in place of spires to scrape the sky.

McAndrew steps from the wheelhouse and points where I am already gazing. 'See that, lad? The *Cutty Sark*, she's called. She'll be some ship when she's finished.'

I turn to him, with my first smile for days. 'She's magnificent now,' I reply, to his evident approval.

''Tis good to sail with a lad who like ships,' he

tells me. 'The last deckhand wanted nothing more than a cheap passage to Glasgow. He jumped ship the moment we touched the wharf. I reckon he was running from something.'

My smile soon vanishes. 'I fear his reason to flee Mull is the same as mine to hasten there,' I tell him. 'They've begun to clear it.'

'Then we're well met. I was going to go back alone – it's easy enough when the weather's fine, for *Sally* has no sails to handle and I know the waters well enough. But having you aboard will save a hundred miles.'

'How so?'

'We'll take the Crinan canal. A nine-mile cut through the top of the Mull of Kintyre. It's short but it's hard work, and I couldn't manage alone. How's your strength?'

'Returning,' I tell him firmly. And it is.

Abby sat in the bathroom, going through her familiar ritual with her new supply of capsules. She was getting faster, but today that made her careless, and she'd not slid the bolt all the way across. The radio's racket masked the rattle at the handle but it seemed to fall suddenly silent as the door burst open.

Abby turned in shock, spilling icing sugar into the bath and scattering capsules all over the floor. If it was her mother she was sunk for sure – but it was Naomi who stepped into the room. Abigail didn't know if this was any better.

Naomi closed and locked the door behind her as she watched Abby scrabble behind the toilet for the spilt capsules. 'It was bad enough having a sister who was a weirdo,' she said. 'Now you're on drugs. Mum and Dad will go mental at this.'

Abigail spun round and stood up, her eyes flashing. 'I'm *not* on drugs. That's the point.' She opened her hand to show the garish capsules. 'I'm taking the zombie-juice out of these horrible things.' She dipped a finger into the icing sugar and held it up. 'And I'm putting this in.'

Naomi just stared at her. Abby put her finger in her mouth and sucked it clean, then held up the bag. 'It's icing sugar, Naomi.'

Naomi frowned. 'But why? I don't understand.'

'Have *you* ever tried being a zombie? Or a robot?'

Naomi said nothing.

'I need one more week. Today's blood test will give me away soon, but there's something I have to finish off first. Please don't tell Mum, Naomi. Please.'

'What is it that's so important?'

Abigail pondered. 'OK,' she said, realising she had to offer something. 'I'll show you – but only if you promise not to say a word. To anyone.'

ॐ

Even at full strength this would be draining toil, but now, after nine of the the locks, I am exhausted. We are dropping again, towards the sea, though we cannot see it yet, and I have no eyes for the scenery.

Each time Captain McAndrew eases his vessel into a lock I must clamber a weed-slippery ladder, carrying two ropes. With these I secure her, bow and stern, then heave the massive lock gate shut behind her. I operate the clanking ratchet to open the sluice gate and let the water out. As the lock empties and his vessel slowly drops from view Captain McAndrew stays aboard to pay out the lines, while I must run back to the previous lock to close the gate, and then ahead, to the next, to open it.

When I return, my lungs and all my muscles burning, it is time to close the sluice and open the gate in front of *Sally*'s bow. I free the mooring lines, coil them carefully, and drop them down on deck as the skipper eases her gently out of this lock and on to the next. I scramble back down the ladder to catch my breath, and prepare myself; for we must repeat this draining duty thirteen times before we reach Crinan basin, where there are men to do it for us. And when at last we arrive there I am heartily glad of it, for my arms and legs tremble with fatigue and sweat soaks my clothes though the day is cold.

'Well worked, lad,' the captain says as he hands me another meal of tea and bacon rolls. We seem to eat nothing else. 'You are indeed eager to return to your island.' And he waves his bacon bun vaguely towards the north-west.

I look about for the first time in hours, suddenly aware how my horizons close in when I am tired. We are moored on the seaward side of the basin, where well-trimmed lawns and neat flowerbeds run up to cosy lock-keeper's cottages. On the opposite side stand the sturdy white walls of the wayfarers' hotel, a building I have seen from afar on a clear day in my former life, before capture and kidnap cut it short.

I look further. Outside the deep sea lock there spreads a wide, calm bay bounded by low headlands. Beyond them, softened by the haze of this spring day, soar the heathered hills of home –

hills I know instantly though I have not seen them for half a year. My heart lifts that after so long I can at last see Mull once more.

⁓

Abigail's mother muted the TV. 'Listen, Dave,' she said.

Her husband looked up from his newspaper. 'What is it?' he asked, half-expecting some unwelcome racket from the street outside or the sound of Muppet destroying another kitchen chair.

Alison's eyes directed his attention upstairs. 'Something we've not heard in ages.'

Dave stared at the ceiling and shook his head. 'I can't hear anything.' Just then came the unmistakable sound of laughter from Abigail's room. *Shared* laughter.

'When was the last time those two did something together?'

'I can't remember.'

'Nearly a year. Before last summer's holiday.'

She turned the TV sound up again. 'It's good to hear,

isn't it? I reckon those tablets are doing Abby the world of good.'

'It's quiet today,' says the skipper, as *Sally* puffs between the headlands and through the tidal race known as the Dorus Mor. All around us the water swells and swirls in evidence of the turbulence under our keel. A huge upwelling, thirty feet across, suddenly appears in front and throws *Sally* violently off course, as if flung aside by some hidden monster. While the skipper works the wheel to bring her back, I hold on and watch as miniature whirlpools twist past our stern, spinning driftwood in our wake.

'I've seen it in a south-westerly gale, against a spring ebb. You wouldn't want to be here then.'

Almost unbalanced by another boil of water, I believe him.

'OK – again,' said Abigail. 'But this time we'll both be serious.'

Naomi checked that the chair still jammed the door shut. Her granny's old bedspread was tucked over the curtain rod to block off the outdoor light and provide a suitable backcloth. She turned the anglepoise lamp so it shadowed Abigail's face as a fireplace might, and then returned to her father's video camera on its tripod.

'Lights. Camera. And action!' She pointed at Abigail who sat, head-bowed, wearing an old linen headscarf and an ancient back-to-front sweater.

Abby raised her eyes to look straight at the camera. When she spoke it was softly, slowly, and with a breathy, lilting accent Naomi recognised but could not place.

This time she did not giggle but watched and listened, amazed to see this other person emerge from within her sister.

Now that I can see it, our progress towards Mull seems painfully slow. We chug past island after island, rocky and grassed, low-lying or heaped up in hills. The captain glories so much in their names that he must point them all out to me on his wheelhouse chart, though I am concerned more to put them behind us than to learn their names. Captain McAndrew shows me the mountains of Jura, the domed summit of Scarba, and on the other side the low lushness of Shuna and Seil. He growls the name of the Garvellachs, and spits out the Corryvreckan. 'A whirlpool of legend, lad, and justly so,' he tells me, pointing at the channel between Jura and Scarba. You can hear its roar ten miles off. I listen, but hear only our engine and the hiss of our bow wave, and step out on to the deck.

There is a sudden change in the engine note, and I look around to the wheelhouse. He eases the regulator further, and steers to starboard as the *Sally* slows. I am struggling to stifle my frustration at this new delay, when the captain hands me a telescope and points to the water.

I see nothing till I raise the glass to my eye and there, dark against the silvery water, is a fin, moving slowly north. I swing the glass and there is another and another, and then a whole group, sinister in their stately progress. I try to count but give up when I reach thirty. I try to guess their size but fear to go on once I am sure each fin stands taller than I do. These are big fish.

'Whales!' I announce. 'Lots of them!'

He takes the glass himself and turn the wheel over to me. Proud as I am to be handed control of a boat such as this, I am soon humbled when he lowers the telescope. 'Those are no whales, lad, but basking sharks. There's no spouts, they don't dive, and they move slowly while they're feeding. Nearly forty of them, I'd say. Let's take a look.'

He throttles the engine up and steers for a point ahead of the school of sharks. Each of them must be twenty feet long or more and could easily stove in our hull if it chose to.

Abby's father opened the door to the computer den, worried by the lack of conflict within. Fiddle music filled the room, and he was astonished to see his daughters – both of them – side by side at the keyboard and working together.

'Declared a truce, have you?' he asked, sceptically. 'Though technically this is the five-minute changeover period when neither of you is supposed to be on the computer.'

'Not so much a truce as an alliance,' said Abigail.

'Then your mother and I are definitely doomed. And that poor machine needs a rest.'

He moved round to see what was on the screen. Musical notation. 'What is it you're doing, anyway?'

'We're laying down a backing track.'

'Oh,' he said. It was only when he was halfway down the stairs that he thought to ask what it was supposed to be backing.

We drift amid the beasts, our engine idling, as the tide takes us north towards Lismore lighthouse. The captain circles the deck, looking down on the pack of huge creatures.

'I've thought about hunting them, you know,' he tells me. 'I've talked to the fishermen, and I've always ended up saying no. They're big, aye, and landing just one of them could yield enough meat and oil to last a village for months. But it's their very size that's the problem. *Sally's* strongly built but I wouldn't back our hull against their thrashing, I tell you. And once you've caught it and killed it, you must get it ashore somehow. Not an easy thing to do. So no, all I've ever done is watch them and wonder.'

And I wonder too, but not about killing them. One of the largest sharks glides by. Its cavernous mouth is held wide open to gather the plankton that make up its diet, and I am sure I could walk in without ducking. The dappled black and silver skin of its back glistens in the spring sunshine, The huge dorsal fin stands proudly, a mere arm's length away; and fifteen feet astern, the tail fin slaps lazily from side to side as the creature and its clan make their stately progress up the Firth of Lorne. I stretch out to brush the tip of the dorsal fin with my fingers, but quickly pull back when I feel how rough the skin is. If the monster notices my contact it gives no sign.

'You're right, lad. Hunting them don't seem fair somehow,' says the captain. He engages the engine gently, and when we are well clear he turns the wheel, opens the regulator, and sets our course for the entrance to the Sound.

Abby reached across the breakfast table for the milk. Her mother grabbed her wrist in one hand and stretched out her fingers with the other. They were splattered with the deep red-brown blotches of sepia ink.

'What's this?' she asked.

Abby retrieved her hand and studied the stains left by last night's letter-writing, as if seeing them for the first time. 'Hmm,' she said. 'It seems be in the dermis rather than on the epidermis, and it's developed overnight. The associated symptoms are: fatigue' – she slumped in her chair – 'and high fever' – she wiped her brow and splashed water on her cheek. 'Coupled with a recent history of travel, I am forced to conclude this can mean only one thing, Lady Mayor: Ebola Fever.'

'Abby, stop this idiocy. Wash that off – whatever it is – and get ready for school.'

'Lady Mayor, this a public-health emergency and –'

Naomi laid her arms on the table. Most of the fingers, the backs of both hands and one wrist were similarly blotched.

'Good Lord!' exclaimed Abigail. 'It's more contagious than I thought!'

Naomi slid from her chair to the floor, where she made gurgling noises, and stared, glassy-eyed, at the ceiling. Milk bubbled from her lips.

'We must impose an immediate and total quarantine!' said Abigail. 'No one enters, no one leaves this building!'

Naomi's gurgling grew louder.

'I concur with my colleague,' said Abigail. 'On no account must anyone enter a school.'

'DAVE!' Mum yelled up the stairs. 'Please come and deal with your daughters. They're nothing to do with me any more.' She stood up, gathered her things and glared at Abigail. 'Sorry, doctor. The mayor's just retired.'

We're past Salen, where the Sound turns north, and Tobermory lies not far ahead. I'm glad the Morvern cliffs are behind us, with their white waterfalls. I cannot see Tobermory yet, hidden as it is behind the bulk of Calve Island, but there is much activity in the Sound outside the bay. Yachts under russet sails tack and gybe round temporary markers, attended by steam boats, and a ferry loaded with spectators and much hung with bunting.

'The regatta,' says the skipper, in answer to my questioning look.

I sigh. Of all the days to return, I have chosen the busiest. The little town will be crawling with police and soldiers and Williams' spies. I can be sure the pier will be watched, and vessels coming in from Glasgow subject to special attention.

'Captain,' I ask him, 'what say you we go in through the Doirlinn?'

He studies me carefully. The main entrance to Tobermory Bay is wide and deep and free of hazards. The Doirlinn is an alternative route, only accessible above half-tide – a narrow channel running close to the rocks and over the masts of a long sunk fishing boat, which legend has turned into a lost galleon of the Spanish Armada.

'What's the line?' he demands.

'Church tower, bearing 239 degrees.'

'And the least depth, just now?'

I know he knows this, but he is testing me. I look at the shore, and judge we are at half-tide, on the flood. The *Sally* draws six feet unladen. 'We'll have a foot or two to spare,' I tell him, sounding more confident than I feel.

'Then very well. And you will be the leadsman, and if you run us aground, or snag us on the galleon, I will string you up as a pirate, boy.'

Abby's parents watched as she headed away to school, helped by Naomi in lugging a strange package neither had wanted them to see.

'I can forgive that quarantine nonsense, Dave, but she's looking so tired this last week. Naomi too. They've been spending hours on that computer, and doing things with feathers and parchment, but they're so secretive about it all.'

'I checked the websites they've been logging on to.'

'Oh?'

'Admiralty charts for Tobermory Bay. Victorian servant costumes. Glasgow–London steam-train timetables. British sea life.'

'I'm none the wiser.'

'Nor me. But whatever they're up to, it's good to see them up to it together.'

We coast through the narrows, dead slow. I cross from side to side, dropping the leadline and calling the depths back to the captain. I hope I'm right about the tide.

The rocks of Calve Island come within spitting distance but I know this is where the water is deeper, as my calls confirm. I check the base of the lead each time I bring it up, to see what kind of sea bed we're passing over. Mud. Again and again mud – thankfully enough, if we are to touch it with our keel.

'Eight feet . . . ten feet . . . two fathoms.' My

calls confirm we are through the Doirlinn. I look up to see the head of the bay teeming with craft of all types in a hubbub of noise and gaiety. I look to the skipper once more. 'I hesitate to make another request –'

'But you wish to be put ashore away from town.' He enjoys watching the surprise on my face 'You hide it well, lad – or should I say lass – but you have a purpose on Mull you wish to conceal from the police and the Army, as you have from me.' He holds up a hand to stop me speaking. 'No. To know what it is would make me an accomplice.'

I am doing no work, but I sweat now anew. To come all this way and be turned over to the police so close to my goal would be bitter indeed. He smiles. 'You have brightened and shortened my passage, whatever your real name. You are a good worker, and you have the makings of a sailor. So yes, I will put you ashore well away from prying eyes.'

He goes on, with a wider smile. 'Besides, I would not wish the ridicule of tying up at the pier to see my deckhand lad arrested as a runaway girl. I could never live here again.'

So we drop anchor in a quiet cove, and he paddles me ashore in his tender. He waves me off and I step on to my island, so much more precious to me now than when I left it. I feel underfoot the stones I have missed for so long; my toes wiggle at the knowledge of it. I smell the pines, and the kelp, and the heather, and I breathe it all in deeply.

Food was passed around the table, but unaccompanied by the usual chit-chat.

'You're a little quieter than this morning, Doctor Jones,' said Abby's mother. 'Everything all right? Busy on call?'

Abby didn't reply. Her mother turned to Naomi, who didn't speak either.

'Your patient too. You've made a rapid recovery from your Elopa Fever, or whatever it was. I thought it was always fatal.'

'Maybe it's the weaker form that just takes the voice away,' said her husband. 'We might get some peace.'

I consider changing into my own clothes but decide against; I will play the boy a little longer yet. I set off up the steep and thickly wooded hillside, away from the town. Dervaig is some miles away, a distance I will have to double if I am to avoid all the houses and people in between.

Near the top of the rise I hear urgent footsteps on a forest path, running hard towards me. Fearing I am discovered already, I crouch low amid the brown bracken and the tangle of mossy birch branches. There is a sudden crashing in the undergrowth behind me and I am flung to the ground, and pinned there by a huge grey wolfhound. Fingal! He is far bigger than I remember, and he threatens to bring down trees with the furious wagging of his tail as he licks my face.

'Fingal?' There is a breathless call from the path nearby. 'Morag?'

I know instantly it is Calum.

Abby looked at her plate and speared a cherry tomato. She looked from one of her parents to the other. 'Mum . . . Dad . . . I've something to tell you.'

Her mum looked at her steadily, but her father rattled on. 'Oh no! You've gone off tomatoes. Broccoli I can understand, but –'

'No. Seriously.' She put her fork down. 'I know you're waiting on a call from the doctor about my medicine. But I can tell you now what the result is.'

'So you are Doctor Jones after all. Or maybe just clairvoyant.'

272

'There's no medicine in my blood. None at all.'

'What?' her mother demanded.

'The blood level will be zero.'

'How come?' Her mother's voice was not rising, as Abigail feared, but this cold, controlled anger was worse.

'I've not taken it for months.'

'But I made sure. Every night I made sure you took it. I didn't once forget.'

Abigail looked directly at her mother, hating to see the hurt in her eyes. 'I emptied the capsules.'

The ketchup bottle slammed down on the table. All the crockery and cutlery jumped and Muppet, sleeping on his mat nearby, woke suddenly and scampered to the safety of the hall.

'You mean you've been tricking us all this time?'

Abby held her mother's gaze as long as she could. 'Yes.'

'WHY? WHY ON EARTH WOULD YOU DO THAT, ABBY?'

Her mother's anger liberated Abby from her guilt. 'Those capsules took part of me away. They shut my windows to other worlds. I missed all that, and I wanted it back.' She stood up, aware for the first time that she was nearly as tall as her mother. 'There's nothing wrong with me. There never was.'

'We decide that, young lady. Us and the doctors. We're going straight back there tomorrow to get a fresh supply of tablets. I will keep them under lock and key, and make sure you take them every night.'

'But Mum –'

'DON'T "BUT MUM" ME!'

'Dad?'

He didn't say anything. Abby turned back to her mother. 'Could you tell? Did you know? You thought I was taking them all along. You said they were working, that I was much better, and the teachers were really pleased. You thought it was the tablets doing that. It wasn't. It was me.'

'She has a point, Alison.'

'Did you know about this?'

'No. Though I did wonder.'

'What about you, Naomi?'

Abigail spoke up in her sister's defence. 'She found out a week ago. I made her promise not to tell.'

Her mother tried another tack. 'You've got exams next week, Abigail. They're important. You can't afford to mess them up.'

Abigail was ready for this. 'Well, I'll certainly mess them up if you start the tablets again now. Remember how they zombified me for the first two weeks last time?'

Abby's father spoke up at last. 'How about a deal, Abby? Do well enough in your exams to prove you don't need the tablets, and we'll discuss it with the doctors. But if you mess them up, and go AWOL in your head like you did before, then there's nothing to discuss. It's back on the tablets and me and Mum will both make sure you take them. What do you say?'

Abigail didn't need to ponder his offer for long. 'Sounds fair enough to me.'

'Alison?'

There was a long long pause, before Abby's mother sat down again. 'I'll think about it.'

Calum and I embrace fiercely. When we release each other we are unable at first to speak, so we laugh, then embrace again, while Fingal scampers around us in tight, excited circles. Calum steps back a moment, as if to confirm I really am wearing trousers. I open my mouth to explain, but he holds up his hand. It is then I notice the scar on the side of his head. It is well-healed but stands out pale in his sunburnt face, a jagged line that runs up under his hairline. I trace it with my finger.

'Was that when . . . ?' I ask him tentatively.

'It was. And the reason I could not come after you. That and my leg. But your mother ministered to both.'

'Tell me everything.'

'Later.' He turns aside. 'We've no time now.' And he sets off in a fast half-walk, half-run, back down the path towards town. I struggle so much to keep up I'm sure his legs have grown longer.

After a time I notice something else: there is a catch in his stride, a limp. It is slight, and it does not slow him down, but it is there.

'They've cleared Calgary,' he tells me bluntly. 'And Croig. Every single tenant forced from their homes and on to the beach.' I have never seen him angry like this. 'They're loading them all on to a ship in Calgary Bay, right now. While Tobermory gentry enjoy their regatta.'

'And Dervaig?' I ask.

He stops to look at me, and nods gravely. 'Dervaig too. I'm sorry, Morag.'

We race on through the thinning woodland as I take this in: that my house is empty and my mother forced on a ship to take her to another world.

'How did you find me?' I ask as we emerge from the wood on to an open ridge. It commands a view of the multicoloured waterfront houses, the ferry pier and the sheltered waters of the bay. Below us crowds throng the streets.

'I sat here, watching every vessel coming in

today. I knew this was the last day you could still be in time. When I saw that puffer come through the Doirlinn and drop anchor far from town, I knew you had to be aboard.'

'What now?'

'Horses.'

We study the horses tethered on the flat ground in front of the distillery. 'That one,' I say, pointing to a large black mare which looks somehow familiar.

'Then I'll take the gelding next to her. The bay. And we'll set all the others loose to aid our escape. Ready?'

'Ready,' I tell him.

We stroll down from the ridge as innocently as we can and quickly untie horse after horse, working towards our chosen mounts. The liberated creatures stand about in puzzled uncertainty, till a shout goes up from the water's edge: 'Hey! You there!' Calum and I untie the rest, and yell and wave our arms till they panic and scatter.

The wide-eyed bay tugs at its reins, and when Calum unties and mounts it he is soon thrown. The horse whinnies, kicks out and runs off, scattering the platoon of red-coated soldiers who now race towards us.

By the time Calum is on his feet I am in the black mare's saddle. I bend to grab his wrist as he reaches up, and between us we manage to bring him up behind me. I pull the reins to turn the horse, and dig my heels into her ribs, just as the first soldier makes a grab for her bridle. We set off at a gallop and race up the steep street, to astonished looks from the top-hatted men and their richly dressed wives descending for the races.

We are soon at the top of the town, and the noise behind us fades, but I know the soldiers will be on our trail before long. I steer the horse off the road and away across the fields. Flocks of sheep part before us like bleating seas. We clear a wall, and then another, in leaps so big it is all I can do to remain in the saddle. How Calum manages without saddle or stirrup I cannot guess, though I know his strong arms around my waist help us both.

The mare's mane flicks my face as I lean low over her neck and urge her onward. Fast as she is, she cannot outrun Fingal, who races alongside, his long grey fur streaming behind and his pink tongue lolling.

'But what's her first name?' asked Naomi, as she and Abigail lie back on the slowly spinning roundabout.

Abigail watched the clouds rotate. 'Miss.'

'Don't be daft.'

'I didn't give her one.'

'Everybody has a first name. And we should know what Miss Wallace's is by the end, when she's come round.'

'Like you have.'

Naomi sat up sharply. 'What?'

'You've come round. You're helping me with this, and I'm glad, but I still don't know why.'

'Don't flatter yourself. Do you want the truth?'

'Of course.'

'You were getting far too goody-two-shoes. When you were a zombie robot and never getting into trouble all the heat was on me. And when they all said your exam results were going to be A1 it got worse. I'd be the one to take the flak. This way we share some of it, and if your project's any good I get some of the credit.'

Abby sat up slowly and looked her sister in the eye. 'You want to know her name?' she said. 'It's Naomi. Naomi Wallace.'

As we near Dervaig we pass croft after croft, all freshly cleared and newly empty. When I see my own home, I nearly fall from the horse. The roof is put in, and flame still flickers from what remains unburnt of the thatch. The whitewashed walls are blackened by smoke, and the few belongings I had in the world are strewn across the grass outside the smashed front door. There is no sign of my mother.

'There's nothing here,' says Calum urgently. 'We must hasten to Calgary. That is where she is.' When I hear a musket shot in the distance I am snapped back into action, and I spur the horse on again.

We make rapid progress over the heather and open grassland, but when I look over my shoulder it is to see a chasing gang of troopers and police riding hard in our pursuit. Fingal and the horse are tiring by the time we first sight the ocean, and my spirits soar to see there is still a ship in the bay. When a sail spills down from her spars I shudder to think we may yet be too late, and I kick the horse into a full-blooded gallop.

We crest a rise above the beach, and see it is studded with people gathered to bid farewell forever to their evicted kin. It is a pitiful spectacle.

The horse plunges madly down the steepening

slope. I give up any attempt to control her and concentrate solely on staying on her back. Somewhere, in the desperate rush of our flight, I find space to think this is familiar, and yet not. Have I not dreamt this? And was I not alone?

Another musket shot, closer now, alerts the people on the beach, who turn away from the ship and the sea to face us. Over their heads I see another sail lowered. There is little wind, but I plead for even that to fall still completely.

We are on the dunes above the beach, and then on the beach itself, and the people part to let us through. With a struggle I bring the horse to a halt. It stamps and whinnies as Calum leaps to the ground.

He looks up at me. 'Go!' he says. 'I will delay them. Go now!' Our eyes lock for an instant, and I know that an ocean may soon separate us forever.

He slaps the horse's rump. It rears and charges into the water, splashing over the waves till it is wading up to its fetlocks and then over them. And swimming in the water beside us is Fingal.

A clanking noise tells me the ship is raising her anchor. There are people at her stern, waving and calling, although not now in farewell. Another musket shot makes me look round to the shore and I see that Calum has marshalled the people into a phalanx to block the beach. As our pursuers approach the people stand firm, arms linked in a defiant fence. There is shouting, and a trooper is pulled from his horse to a loud cheer. The beach descends into a chaotic brawl.

I halt the horse. The water is up to her belly and over my ankles. 'Calum!' I scream. 'Come with me! What is there now to stay for?'

He stands at the water's edge. I cannot tell if he hears, and if he does, whether he will heed me. 'Calum!' I shout again. The ship's bell starts a continuous ringing and the anchor clanks again. The moment will soon be gone.

When I look back to the beach I see him

running through the water towards me. First he splashes, then he wades, and then he swims, till he reaches me, as I force the horse into deeper water. The sea is freezing around my knees, and the panicky horse is increasingly hard to control.

The ship is not far off but its anchor is now up, and wind begins to fill the sails. The shouting at the stern rail grows louder and more urgent, and I see a rope ladder lowered from the deck.

'Swim yourself!' says Calum, 'Forget the horse!' I hesitate, but only a moment, before I slip from the saddle to join him. The horse turns back for the safety of the beach, and Calum and I swim side by side in a desperate race for the ship.

Icy seawater clamps my chest and draws the strength from my arms, and I feel myself slowing. The ladder hangs tantalisingly close, but I fear I cannot reach it, and I know that if I do not I cannot make it back ashore.

It is then I hear, from the stern rail high above, and clear amid all the tumult aboard and ashore, a voice I have known all my life: the voice of my mother. I look up to see her face and her outstretched, urging arms. 'Morag!' she cries. I kick out and force myself on, and as my legs grow numb I stretch out my hand, till at last I have the ladder in my grasp.

I hang there, unable to move, clinging to one side of the ladder while Calum clings to the other. We hold Fingal between us. As the ship gathers speed sailors scuttle down the ladder to haul us upward. Rough hands pass me over the rail and into the arms of my mother. None of us can speak, but we are safe and we are together – she, Calum, Fingal and me. I cannot ask for more.

Epilogue

I am not a whale . . . Abby chanted to herself as the last of the many little buttons were glued to her head. *I am not a whale*. She studied the multicoloured wires that ran from the buttons to a silver metal box the size of a CD walkman. She wasn't sure if it was already recording, but the idea that her thoughts might, at any moment, slide along those wires to betray her daydreaming was enough to make her focus intently on the here-and-now of the EEG room.

Dr Bolton handed her a large black belt, with a kind of leather holster. 'Buckle up,' she said, and she slipped the metal box into the holster.

'How long?' asked Abby.

'Twenty-four hours. All your brainwaves, awake and asleep, till this time tomorrow. Starting . . . now!' She pressed a button on the box, then closed the holster.

'Just go about your daily life as normally as you can.'

That's easy for you to say, thought Abby, as she looked in the mirror. Her head was covered by twenty little buttons and masses of wiring. *I've got to walk around looking like this. And no daydreaming for a whole day and night.*

Dr Bolton turned to Abby's mother. 'Mrs Jones, if you notice Alison – sorry, Abigail – go AWOL, as she puts it, just press this button here. It marks the recording so we can see what her brainwaves are doing at the time.'

'It's not going to happen,' said Abby. *I'll make sure of it*, she thought.

'Let's hope so,' said the doctor, but with a tone that indicated she'd be disappointed if her tests turned out normal. And Abby heard something else: she'd be disappointed because it showed she'd got it wrong first time around, though she'd never admit it.

Abby's father picked up on it too. 'If nothing shows she can stay off the tablets, can she?' he asked.

'Yes.'

'And does that mean she ever needed them?'

'Mr Jones, you saw the trace last time. It was quite unmistakable. If it's normal now it can only mean that she's grown out of her condition.'

I never had a condition at all, Abby thought. There was no point saying it.

Calum and I sprawl side by side on the deck, panting and drenched, like fresh-caught herring. Passengers rush off in search of blankets and dry clothes. Fingal stretches full length on a patch of sun-warmed wood, content to dry off in his own good time.

Questions burst from my mother's mouth, tumbling over each other so urgently that none is completed. 'Morag, my silver darling! How did you – when – who –?' She stops for an instant when she sees my trousers, and her smile widens. 'And whose are those?'

Abby dawdled through the windy park, throwing sticks for Muppet, while she waited for Naomi to return from the shops. For the hundredth time she looked around and checked that the hood of her sports top hid every one of the wires that festooned her head. Kids were gathering by the bus shelter again, Elaine among them, and Abby was sure she'd been spotted. *Any more than three of them and I'll take the long way home*, she thought.

But when Naomi joined her at last, flicking through her new magazines and obviously eager to get home to read them, Abigail knew she couldn't back out. 'I don't know why you're so keen to get your comics every Wednesday,' she said. 'It's the same stuff every week.'

Naomi smiled. She wasn't going to rise to this. 'That's exactly why I have to have them,' she said, as she strode towards the park exit and the bus shelter beyond it.

Along with the other passengers we watch as first Mull, and then Coll and Tiree slip astern, to dissolve into the horizon haze behind us. We all know, though none of us says, that we will never again see these shores. Calum settles to sleep under a pile of blankets, with Fingal for a pillow.

I am weary to my bones, but sleep will not come. My mother and I look west, along the length of the ship, to the dark Atlantic, to Canada, to our future. Although we have an ocean of talking ahead we are both already hoarse from filling in the missing months since we were parted.

By the time they passed the bus shelter there were five kids inside. Abby called Muppet to her, but as she bent to snap his lead to his collar the wind caught her hood and flipped it down, exposing all the wires and buttons on her head.

The shelter fell suddenly quiet for a moment, before a gale of laughter blew out. 'She really *is* turning into a robot!' cackled Elaine. As the laughter loudened and closed in around her Abigail felt her face flush hot and red, and heard the blood pound in her ears. Desperate though she was to escape, embarrassment fixed her to the spot, facing her tormentors as an exhausted deer might a hungry wolf-pack. 'A red-nosed robot!' they screeched, working up for the kill.

Muppet tugged at his lead and Naomi urged her onward. 'Ignore them,' she said.

'Look!' Elaine pointed at the steady green light on the EEG box clipped to Abigail's belt. 'She's on standby!' But as the cruel laughter rang again in Abby's ears, an idea came to her.

She looked at Naomi, and something passed between them. Her finger hovered over the button on the box.

'No!' Naomi called. 'You know what the doctor said. It's dangerous if you press it when you don't need to.'

Abigail nodded and looked at Elaine. 'I know. And not just for me.'

Naomi turned to Elaine, and then her friends, subtly positioning herself between them. 'If she presses that button, keep well clear,' she said in an urgent whisper. '*Anything* might happen.'

Elaine sniggered. Abigail held her in her gaze as she punched the button, despite Naomi's pleading cry. The steady green light turned into a flashing red one, and a shiver ran through Abigail's body. Her breath came in loud hissing gurgles as she lurched forwards with a stiff-kneed gait.

Elaine hesitated now, and her friends drew back in fearful silence. When Elaine too tried to retreat she found her path blocked by Naomi. An unearthly moan emerged from somewhere deep within Abigail and she stumbled closer, her arms raised and fingers curled claw-like before her. Saliva frothed at her mouth.

'Stop her!' Elaine cried, with a tremor in her voice.

Naomi shook her head. 'I can't. Not when she's like this.'

Elaine tried to squirm past. 'Then let me through!' she pleaded.

Naomi wrapped her arms around Elaine's chest and held her pinned in place. Again she shook her head. 'Can't do that either,' she said. 'I'm only safe if she gets you first.'

Abigail bared her teeth and clamped her fingers round Elaine's throat. 'Stop her!' screeched Elaine, wild-eyed and thrashing. 'Please! I didn't mean it! I was joking!'

Abigail transformed in an instant. The breathing noises stopped, her hungry snarl turned into a smile, and her arms fell to her side. 'Me too,' she said quietly, as she pressed the button again and the light returned to green. 'But some jokes aren't funny.'

Naomi released Elaine, who looked around in vain for support from her friends. All they did was stare. Naomi met their gaze, one by one. 'She's not a robot,' she said levelly. 'She's not a weirdo.' She turned again to Elaine. 'She's my sister. Understand?'

Away to the south the distant loom of Skerryvore lighthouse sweeps the evening sky, the last evidence of land until we strike Newfoundland. I find within me the question we both know is coming. 'Mother?' I ask.

'Yes, Morag.' She wraps her shawl tighter round her shoulders.

'Colonel Williams. He knew Mull. He was stationed there. He knew you. And he came for me.'

'Yes.' She turns to look at me, and then towards the ship's bow and whatever lies beyond. The lighthouse glow reveals her face, but the deep pools of her eyes are still in shadow. There is a long pause – two full sweeps of the lighthouse beam – before she turns back to me. 'Morag, let me tell you of your father.'

Abigail sat with Naomi and her parents in the school hall

for the end-of-year Celebration. She clutched the precious tickets her mother had given her that morning and which she'd read and re-read ever since, the tickets that boldly announced her holiday destination the following day: Canada. 'A kind of reward,' her mother had said.

The headmaster droned on and on about sports teams and community service and the new science block. Abigail wasn't listening: she was mapping, in her head, the route Morag took across Newfoundland, determined that she would get her family to follow it. She looked up and brought herself back to the room, when the headmaster paused. He was looking at her.

'I do not like to single pupils out at events of this sort,' he said pompously, 'for all of our students are special.' Naomi groaned as he went on. 'And that is why this is a Celebration and not a Prizegiving. But there is one student I do wish to name and to commend as an example to us all. Abigail Jones has overcome a great deal to complete – with a little help from her sister Naomi – an Imagination Project that is simply stunning.

We're putting the whole thing on display – the songs, the diaries, the letters and tickets and charts – and right now we're going to show you how the video part of the project begins.'

There was a stir in the hall as electric blinds rolled down and the lights dimmed. A projection screen unrolled on the stage, and the video projector flickered into life.

On the screen a grainy and unsteady image formed – an image of a young girl who was, at one and the same time, both recognisably Abby and also someone else, someone from a different time and a distant place. The hall fell silent as she looked out from the screen and began to speak, in an unfamiliar breathy lilt.

'It is a velvet night – windless, warm and still – and we drift, Calum and I, in his father's old boat, on the waters of Bloody Bay. We sprawl, he in the bow, me in the stern. The lines between us are unattended, for the fishing is fruitless tonight . . .'

EGMONT PRESS: ETHICAL PUBLISHING

Egmont Press is about turning writers into successful authors and children into passionate readers – producing books that enrich and entertain. As a responsible children's publisher, we go even further, considering the world in which our consumers are growing up.

Safety First
Naturally, all of our books meet legal safety requirements. But we go further than this; every book with play value is tested to the highest standards – if it fails, it's back to the drawing-board.

Made Fairly
We are working to ensure that the workers involved in our supply chain – the people that make our books – are treated with fairness and respect.

Responsible Forestry
We are committed to ensuring all our papers come from environmentally and socially responsible forest sources.

For more information, please visit our website at
www.egmont.co.uk/ethicalpublishing